Does Common Sense Still Exist??

OR IS EVERYONE Just STUPID (Guillable) !!!!!

George Tremtsidis

1: Life: What is it all about? And how are you going to live it.......

2: Work: The majority of your life and will you make a difference....

3: Government: A democracy, Who do they work for, and why do they exist....

4: Taxes: Why do we pay them, and When is enough, enough!!?

5: Daily Activities: Make sure you do something you enjoy that also benefits your health.

6: World Politics: One World Order, One World Power...

7: Wokeness: How did we get here? The difference between right and wrong is to have an opinion!

8: Climate Change: Someone better tell the truth because everyone is lying!!

9: Inflation: Why does it exist, and does anyone really care!!!

10: Vices: Drug, Alcohol, and Big Pharma: We all have one or two, control and deal with them.

11: Middle-Life(Crisis): Don't forget what's important.

12: Retirement: Start early and educate yourself; don't rely on others!

My Top 10 Common-sense Phrases: I either made them up or heard them over my lifetime.

1: Common-sense exists, but it isn't developed

2: Stock Markets don't just move; they are moved!

3: You can't out-think people who just don't think!

4: Worrying is praying for things you don't really want!

5: Live one day at a time; don't live in the past!

6: You can't pick your family, but you can choose your friends!

7: Crawl before you learn to walk in business as well!

8: Watch your pennies; the dollars will watch themselves!

9: Stay in your lane, don't veer off! Life is way too short!

10: It takes less muscle to smile than it is to frown; try it!

TABLE OF CONTENTS

1: LIFE 1

2: WORK 18

3: GOVERNMENTS 29

4: TAXES 52

5: DAILY ACTIVITIES 69

6: WORLD POLITICS 75

7: WOKENESS AND IT'S STUPIDITY?? 88

8: CLIMATE CHANGE?? GLOBAL WARMING??.... 105

9: INFLATION 120

10: VICES: DRUG, ALCOHOL, AND BIG PHARMA 130

11: MID-LIFE (CRISIS).................................... 141

12: RETIREMENT: 148

SUMMARY AND LAST THOUGHTS?...................... 159

EPILOGUE 163

DEDICATION

Dedicated to my son, and the most important person who
came into my life, Mya.

PERSONAL

This is a book that discusses what you are thinking but scared to say, especially in public. Common sense thoughts that stupid people can't or don't want to understand. As my father used to tell me, "You can't out think those who aren't thinking." I think that saying really magnifies the time we are currently living in.

I will talk about life and how we go through life, the experiences we all have, and the frustration that we all encounter with no way to express ourselves because we are expected to be good little citizens and shut up and pay our taxes and keep paying your taxes til you die. The highs and lows of life and the journey we will all take, and we truly are connected through the six degrees of separation.

This is a book really about your life and how you should handle these frustrations. I want to sum this up by saying all you have to do is take it one day at a time.

As my father used to say, "You can only live one day at a time," so enjoy the journey. There will be a lot of ups and a lot of downs—a lot of doors that will open and a lot of doors that will close. You will meet a lot of good people and some not so good. But if you are lucky enough to make a couple of good friends, hold on to them tight, because aside from your family, you really have no one, except those 1 or 2 people you can really call your friend.

Once you go through the phases, from going to school, graduating if you are lucky enough, getting a job, finding a profession that works, maybe even getting married, and perhaps even having a family, you will realize time has passed so fast, that you wonder where it went.

Hence, the expression I stated above, enjoy the journey and try, every single day, to do something that matters to you and your family, and always, I truly mean this, always be a good person, because if you are, you are making someone else's day, and this world a better place to live in.

Good luck!!

I am going to discuss a number of life topics that I mentioned above and possibly will cross some topics once or twice within each area because your life isn't a straight line but a maze and a web of activities and interactions that have their ebbs and flows throughout your life.

Don't get frustrated with this; just enjoy the read because I guarantee you can relate to most, if not all, of the topics I touch on in this book. It gets really serious and a little silly because if you can't look at some of these topics through a comedic window, you will probably lose your mind.

Please always remember that life is worth living, and we all make mistakes, and most of us learn from these mistakes, but please, I plead with you, don't make the ultimate mistake because if you are reading this book, you can pass this on to the next generation, so they can really enjoy the fruits of this life. They can add positivity to society if they are shown how and why, so please teach the youth the proper way to live life and always to be a good person, even when it doesn't feel right because being a good person will always contribute to a better way of life. You will see it and feel it within yourself, especially on those days when you need a little help.

Also, please remember that you should only live for today. As the saying goes, yesterday has passed, and it can not be changed, so live for today, as tomorrow has yet to come. Live in the moment, not in the future; not that it hurts if you sometimes dream about the future, but remember that today is all we have, so live, experience, grasp, and love it.

So here we go, and don't forget to Enjoy the journey!! Common-Sense does exist, but it may be hard to find!! LOL

1: LIFE

These are some of the oldest questions in history. Where did we come from, and why are we here? But I am not here to answer them because this is not a book about philosophical history or astrophysics. It's a book about life and common sense—if it still exists—and how we got to where we are now. So please keep that phrase in mind when you read each chapter because that is the premise of what this book is trying to communicate to its readers and the world, if possible lol.

So you wake up in the morning and are getting ready for your day. You turn on the TV, and then you hear one shot, two knifed, multiple vehicle accident on the highway, and you wonder WHY? Or are you now numb to it and just going through the motions when you continuously keep hearing this type of news each and every day? You keep hearing this when you turn on the TV and try to grab a coffee before you embark on the daily journey—work, life, balance, yes. Please remember that phrase, as it may be your best friend if you remember it, and implement it in your daily routine.

Why is it that all we hear on the morning news is these types of headlines and stories? I guess the old news saying, "If it bleeds, it leads," is prevalent and still true, as I guess that is how they pay their bills also. I wish sometimes, all of these stations think about when and how they broadcast these stories. Are these the stories that they should be starting within the AM so as to set our mindsets and our days, as some of us really take them to heart? Do they not realize that these stories impact most of us for the entire day!! If they tried to lead with more positive stories or items, maybe we wouldn't have so many issues, such as road rage, mad people, or other items like this. TV and radio stations should review this policy and report on more relevant topics and items because don't we all know that a car accident causes traffic? Really genius?? Or, as I stated above, someone shot, and then they say something like: "Aren't guns illegal in Canada?" So how and why are guns so prevalent, and why are people using them, but nothing seems to happen to these people? If Guns are illegal in Canada, how are these people getting them, or Is that a common-sense question too sensitive to ask these days? Why doesn't Canada have a second amendment like the USA does? Then, we at least can reason with how and why guns are so readily available.

That expression in life, "Take it one day at a time," or it's overwhelming, is really prevalent in today's times, especially what we have gone through over the past three years of shutdowns and alienation from human contact. If you think about life at the holistic level, boy, it's short, and it moves fast. I remember like it was yesterday, being in middle school, and now I am on the tail end of my life. Don't you feel that way, and aren't you supposed to become more rounded and experienced? Yet you keep wondering if you are the only one feeling that way and if you are the only one with Common sense when you look at life and its ups and downs. Life moves so fast, with or without you living in the moment. You are better off living life than thinking about living it. Participate and be active before it's too late and you develop regrets for not living it. Express yourself and your feelings even if you feel you may not be in the mainstream of thoughts or opinions, as this is how we all grow as people by listening to others with different viewpoints.

Maybe you are the only that cares and gives a crap. Maybe everyone else cares but doesn't show it, or perhaps they don't and are living life like it's supposed to be lived, one day at a time. Don't give a crap about tomorrow. Why are you saving anything for a rainy day, and why do you have any life insurance? Because when you are gone, this life, as we know it, is really over. We are told daily to save for our retirement whenever possible. I will discuss this topic a little later, yet when we start doing that, it appears it's never enough, and it's always so far away. Now or for then.

Life, at times, is difficult. If you are married, have kids, own a house, or have a job, do you ever wonder how the hell you make it work each and every single day? Pay the bills, cut the grass, take out the trash, get the kids' lunch ready, pick them up, take them to clubs and team sports events, get breakfast, lunch, and dinner ready? Wow, do you ever wonder how you deal with all of this daily stress without cracking? But some of us do crack and break because we feel we are not getting ahead, especially when the government keeps taking more from us to waste it on stupid and non-COMMON-SENSE nonsense ideas: the good and the bad of everyday life. Well, the majority of us think it's what life is all about. We have family and friends, or people we call friends until the following happens: we don't deal with enough every day, and then this.

How many of you have had this happen to you? Your family member calls you to have a chat about LIFE. You say, what about LIFE? And the conversation goes like this, "You know things are tough and sometimes tight, with money and all, and I am wondering and hoping that, like, maybe, you can lend us some money," AND you say, "You and your wife both work and make a good income? Don't you, from what you tell us? And he says, Yes, so why do you need to ask for money, and he says, bills are piling up. You say you both drive expensive cars and live in a huge house. Why don't you downsize or get less expensive cars? And he says, are you going to give me a loan? I don't need a lecture. And you say, "Do you know what common sense is and what living within your means?" But why do all your family and "friends" think you are doing better than them and need to come to you for help? Don't we all live in the same world? Do you think I am stupid? I watch Judge shows on TV like you do when they need to sue the person they made a loan to. Why do people need to "Keep up with the Jones" as the expression goes? A lot of people are too busy thinking they are living life, and everything sometimes catches up with them. This is somewhat understandable; as I stated above, a lot of things are going on daily if you are married, have kids, own a house and a car or two, and work full-time for a company that doesn't really care about you, especially when push comes to show, and they lay you off.

But why is it that you try to be as responsible as you can and even dream sometimes about winning the lottery or going on that expensive trip, but then, you shake your head, and reality strikes you right between the eyes, and then your "Family" asks for help? Why do you appear to be the only one with any "COMMON SENSE" and responsible, and everyone else seems not to give a crap? They keep chasing the elusive big payday or some other get-rich-quick scheme, and then, they ask for help. EVERYONE, Wake up; there is no "GET RICH QUICK SCHEME," and if there were one, all of those crooks wouldn't be in jail for trying to sell you these schemes. Do you remember Tom Vu or Don Lapre with all the hot girls and fast boats, telling you that this could be you if you just send them some money to read some bogus book or place a couple of ads in a newspaper and people will pay to money, or Bernie, what's his name, who promised 10, 15, 20% return on your money, until everyone, found out it was a Ponzi scheme, one of the largest ever, which put so many people into poverty? That is just to name a few of these geniuses. Now we have this kid who supposedly stole millions by selling crypto dreams that don't really exist, only to find out that it was all a big scam. Why does it always appear that the average Joe, like me, doesn't use their COMMON SENSE when they need to but are always dreaming of all of these ways to have a better life? Don't tell me you aren't one of them. Just use some COMMON SENSE by putting a few dollars away every week, and you will be very surprised what it will turn out to be when you really need some extra fun money. Hard work and smart decisions really do pay off in the long run. People use some COMMON-SENSE; there are no get-rich-quick scams unless you win the lottery.

Let's move on to all those "friends" you have made. You figure you go through life, meeting people while some come and go and others seem to hang around. Have you ever figured out why some people come and go and others don't? Well, when you think about that, you realize you attract people who have the same or similar temperament or possible interests as yourself. Most of these people also have the same thought process as you—COMMON SENSE or what you think is this gene. Think about it. Who can tolerate you except you? Your spouse, at times, can't even stand to be in the same room as you. Most of us have probably experienced this over the past three years during the pandemic, where we spent WAY TOO much time with the same people who we all drove crazy. So the expression, opposites attract, is garbage; you attract the same people as yourself. Do people have explicit characteristics and interests? Of course. Do they like some different things than yourself? Of course. But their main philosophies, thoughts, and cares are usually similar to yours. COMMON SENSE and similar goals in life. If they are not, you are probably unfortunate and have gone through a separation. That's what attracts them to you and you to them. We are told you only make 1 or 2 true friends in life. Is that true? Of course, it is. Think about it. Aside from your family, name how many people you call friends and how many you can truly count on. I am not talking about acquaintances, but true, real friends that you can call at any time of the day to ask for help. If you have more than 2, then you have succeeded in life, or you have something truly special between them and yourself. You truly have. Life is so busy that living it doesn't give you enough time, or you don't make enough time to share it with too many other people other than your family. Take a test next time someone calls you to invite you somewhere. How many times do you instantly say, 'Yes?' Probably at first, then when they explain the underlying reason for the invite, don't you second guess your answer, and how many times do you try to figure out an excuse or a reason why you can't attend. You realize so and so will be there, or you need to contribute to some cause, or you need to be the designated driver. Well, take your invite and shove it unless you want to go for a beer and shoot the shit, as the expression goes, with the 2 of us or maybe a third wheel. Do you ever wonder if the person that invites you to some event ever thinks about it or uses any common sense to realize, why would I ask them, unless there is something in it for me!!! Usually, when you get invited to an event, that doesn't make sense; it's because more people are needed to deflect conversations at this so-called event or occasion. A lot of people want more people around them because they want to seem like they know a lot of people or consider themselves important. So why do we all seem to get sucked into this type of situation until it's too late to say NO? Use some COMMON SENSE people. Don't just go places for the sake of going; go because you really want to go, and when and if you go, bring yourself there and be attentive. Share yourself with people, and don't be reserved and intimidated. Become a person in that environment as someone people want to be around. Make yourself a friendly person, put your wall down, and share yourself and your thoughts. Or if you don't, DON'T GO!!!! Like I stated earlier, life is short, so why do something and spend time doing something you don't really want to do? Do it because you want to do it and be with those people.

Let's move on from the friend's angle to the cost of living. Why the heck does it cost so much for everything? Things have gone crazy in the Western world in terms of prices for everything. Let me ask you, since we are paying so much for a simple coffee, if this ever happened to you, which suggests where people are in their lives. Have you ever been in line trying to order a simple BLACK coffee and you are behind the soccer mom who is on their phone, and when it's their turn to order, they tell the person behind the counter, "Just a sec, I don't know yet," and they keep talking on their phone, for the next, say 5 minutes, until someone behind her says some like, "Do you mind but we need to go to work" and they look at that person like, "EXCUSE ME." How about a like common sense and respect for your fellow human being, Bitch.!! You ever feel like you are in the movie Falling Down with Michael Douglas, and everyone else besides yourself doesn't seem to understand life or have any common sense, like the movie where Michael goes into a fast food restaurant and wants to order a simple breakfast sandwich and the restaurant at just that minute switches to only serve lunch, even though you are a whole 1 minute past the cut-off time for breakfast. So, what did the restaurant do with all the breakfast eggs that were pre-cooked? Do you ever wonder why so many restaurants NOW serve breakfast most of the day, and if this movie has something to do with this because COMMON sense really needs to be more prevalent in life, more often than not!? Why can't Michael just get a breakfast sandwich, geez, and then snap like a lot of people do because all they want to do is deal with people like them, who have COMMON-SENSE? You think that more people should appreciate life and respect their fellow humans, but most couldn't give a crap about you because they are late for that movie or nail appointment. These people that think their life is so much more important than yours are the people that cause more pain for you. They are the ones that crash into your car and start another pain in your ass in life that you need to deal with. Like you didn't have enough on your plate before this jerk came into your life, unwanted, so abruptly. Does anyone have any common, or are they all just stupid.!! You may want to watch that movie with him and really think about it. It really is a metaphor for life, how it should be lived, and how we should act around our fellow human beings. How we should treat people and how we should expect people to treat us.

Like I just stated, this jerk crashes into you because they are rushing to get to some stupid appointment or meeting, and now you need to call the insurance company to report the accident and figure out what the heck that insurance salesman actually sold you in regards to that mandatory insurance policy the government mandates you to buy at sky high prices, that you may never use. "What the hell, what do you mean, I am not covered for a rental car?" because the person who hit my car didn't have any insurance and wasn't supposed to be in the country. They say, "Didn't YOU READ YOUR POLICY?" And you say, "WHAT, who reads the fine print after the first ten pages?" Yes, it is true, there is NO COMMON SENSE in the insurance business, and GOD helps you if you ever have to deal with the "INSURANCE COMPANY." But the government makes it mandatory, as I said, and illegal to not have insurance for your car, and they charge you the premium for insurance based on where you live, as opposed to your record or driving history and ability. WTF are they talking about? I have never had an accident, but my rates keep going up; why? Because you moved into a very bad claims neighborhood!!! Crazy!! Is everyone here losing their minds, or is it just me?? Where did the common sense of ability and driving history go for insurance premiums? I will tell you where it went. It went out the window with all of these lobbyists and greedy CEO's that think they can get away with it, and when they are caught, all they seem to say is, "WE ARE SORRY" for trying to screw you all!!!

I will give you an example that occurred to me. So, I had to go on a business trip. I did this on a regular basis like most of you do or did, and this time, at the airport, the self-park was closed due to weather and flooding issues, so the only thing opened was valet parking. Not giving this a second thought, I pulled up, gave them my keys, and ran to catch my flight again, thinking nothing of it. That is until I returned from my 5-day business trip. Exhausted, I went to retrieve my car from valet, as I had never done this previously at the airport, and while waiting for about 20 – 30 minutes, I asked the attendant, "What's going on?" They said that it's busy and they would be with you in a few more minutes; please be patient. After being " PATIENT" for another 15 minutes, I got a little anxious and went back to ask. This time, I am told, sorry, but " We are having an issue locating your car"? Hmmmm, really, what does the F!@!@!? Does that mean? A few minutes later, some dude shows up and throws me the keys. After paying $200 for parking using the valet, which I had no choice, instead of the $100 for self-part, I went to my car, opened the trunk, threw in my carry on to the trunk, and then went to open my front door, and guess what the 'F' I see??

Well, let me tell you, my car had been ransacked. What do I mean? Well, there are a number of papers thrown around, my middle console armrest was torn out and sitting on the floor, and my dash-cam, and everything and anything that is valuable was stolen. What the F!!? I called the manager, and he said, "SORRY, sir. We are not responsible for any damages to your car! Look at your claim ticket!" What do you do now? You can throw a fit, which would solve NOTHING, or you jump in your car and try to figure it out until you realize everything inside your car is stolen, and now you need to deal with, wait for it, the INSURANCE Company and or the police for a report for the insurance company. You call the police to put in a report and get a report number, and they say, "Sorry, sir, that is private property, and by the way, there were a number of vandalized cars this weekend at the airport. We can fill out the report for your insurance company if you need to, but we can't do anything else for you as the video surveillance cameras were "NOT WORKING" this past week." How convenient? Now comes the fun part, because no one cares or gives a shit, you need to think about what was in your car the HONEST way, and boy, does your head start to spin and hurt when you realize what you have lost. That's if you can even remember what was in your car. Everything from pictures of your kids to expensive items that sometimes you leave in your car when you shouldn't, such as your extra watch, customized pen and pencil set, and things that should never have been in your car but because we are all busy trying to pay our overtaxed lives. As most sales reps can attest to, we live in our cars if we are professionals at our job. We also need anything and everything to be in our cars, just in case!!

Now, you call the insurance company to report the claim. They ask you questions that put your integrity to the forefront, like, Yeah buddy, I broke into my own car and ripped out the middle console, and broke a number of other items in MY CAR because I want to claim $2-3,000, before my $1000 deductible. Not to mention, I brought my car in to be fixed and lost it for 4-5 days without a car rental as it was not included in the stupid policy you sold me. "DO YOU HAVE ANY COMMON SENSE, or are you JUST STUPID " like the rest of the morons out there in your industry that think everyone is out to score an insurance claim, GENIUS! Yeah, I want to rip you guys off because I have only been paying $ 1,500 for car insurance for the last 35 years, for a total of over $50k in premiums, and I want to get maybe three grand back. Yeah, maybe I am the one that is STUPID without any COMMON SENSE, that's it, yeah. You freakin moron. I can't make this shit up. Trust me. But again, maybe it happened to you. Life! Sometimes, it's hard to deal with, but keep going because it's worth living.

Has this ever happened to you, and then you wish you actually did put in that $10k Rolex watch or those $4000 golf clubs into the claim and tell these assholes they were in the car also. But not me, because I am honest and have, wait for it, COMMON SENSE, morals, and some decency!! Idiot me. Prove they weren't, you idiot! OR do you do what I did, tell the truth, and get the third degree from the insurance company because you were honest and just really wanted to fix your car because you ripped the leather seats up and ripped out your door sides because you were having a bad. IDIOTS!! Well, I tell ya, I wish I did because, again, NO ONE CARES, NO ONE HAS ANY COMMON SENSE, and pretty much are PRETTY STUPID in life. Next time, let me tell you what I would do, or should I not, just in case some adjuster is reading this book. YOU ARE AN IDIOT. I will leave it at that. OOPS, sorry, thanks for that $1700 check after the deductible. Oh, by the way, what the F is a deductible. Why is there a deductible? You pay for insurance, and then you need to pay them more for them to interrogate you and then possibly cut you a smaller cheque, and WAIT FOR IT, "INCREASE YOUR PREMIUMS AT YOUR NEXT RENEWAL" Does that even make sense? You buy insurance because it's mandated by the geniuses in the government, and then when you use it, not only do they charge you a premium, "A   DEDUCTIBLE" !! They increase your rates, not because you caused an accident, but because someone vandalized your car without you being there or even better, SOMEONE racing to the Beauty or nail salon hit you because you were on your way home, working to pay for the insurance which is mandatory from the morons in government. What the F? Does anyone have ANY COMMON SENSE, or is EVERYONE JUST STUPID!! Or is it just me!! I think sometimes it is me, and I shouldn't be in this lane of life as none of it at times makes any sense, or I should say COMMON SENSE to me.

Since we are speaking of drivers, specifically stupid and incompetent drivers, do you ever wonder how some people get their licenses or why they get their licenses? Is there any common sense with the driving instructor? How can they pass someone who doesn't look in their blind spot, check their rear-view mirror, or doesn't even put on their blinker to change lanes? Did we forget what the basic skills that are needed to drive are? No, we are just being stupid and money-hunger for taxation purposes and to make insurance companies ever-richer. We have individuals who go to remote areas to pass their driver's test in this province because they couldn't pass the test in a congested part of a busy city. They drive over 100km away because they don't have the skill set, and they won't be able to pass the test in high traffic or stressful situations. Why is this even allowed when it is reported regularly to the authorities and in the news by these remote communities, and no one even checks into it? Because no one wants to offend anyone anymore, as we all have to be politically correct, and no one really gives a crap. No one wants to be called a stereotypical racist by demographically pointing out who these people are who are going this far to obtain a driver's license. If driving testing facilities were held accountable for approving new drivers' actions, do you think they would give it a second thought by passing that individual who drove, say, 200 km to take their driving test in Northern Ontario instead of Toronto, or even have someone with a fake ID go take that test for them? Where is the common sense and accountability? Well, let me tell you, there isn't any because all these government-appointed employees only care about a couple of things, and one of them is just getting by and hopefully collecting that lucrative pension that is promised to them at retirement. If we held them accountable, say, for this instructor passing someone, and say, this person, next day, has a major accident, do you think that this would make them more accountable at their job? Let's hold people in power more accountable, and let's see what happens in life. I will tell you that a lot of things would change and things in my opinion would get a lot better.

At least one level of government is doing the right thing when it comes to not fleecing its citizens. It's the Ontario provincial government, which in 2021 agreed to waive sticker renewal charges. Why do we need to pay $120 each and every year to buy a sticker for a car that basically lets you drive on the road, which is paid for and has been paid for many times over by my taxes, and verifies the mandatory insurance that I am told I must have before I can drive on the tax paid roads. This government finally did something that makes SENSE common sense by waiving this sticker fee because we don't pay enough taxes. We pay for our license, sticker fees, and insurance. This topic, TAXES, will be discussed in length throughout the book and in one chapter in full detail. Please, give some more back to us, MR Government, because after all, it's my hard-earned money that you continue to take and waste, and in most cases, for no apparent reason, that you can give me for taking my money, except to give some back at times, when you find it convenient, such as when its election time. IDIOTS!!!

You try to live life with a sense of decency and morals, and all you have to show for it is more work, less take-home pay, and more taxes because no one cares about you because you are part of the middle class. God forbid that you make a bit too much money, not a lot more, but just a bit more, because you want to better your family, and they, the greedy bureaucrats, now take more. Then they turn around and say, you don't qualify for this or that tax credit, or you don't qualify for a discounted rate here or there because you are middle class, and how dare you ask!!! COMMON SENSE, think not!! You better just pay and shut up, you middle-class person, as you really don't mean anything to us except when it's election time.

I know a lot of people who have children with special needs, but because they make just a little too much money, again, not enough to be considered high earners, but just enough to make them NOT qualify for the disability benefits, they should get, and which their kids are entitled to, which receive absolutely nothing to help these kids with their disabilities. Wages and earners in this society seem not to be tolerated because god forbid, you try to provide a little more for your family. But those non-accountable government workers know better, don't they? Have you ever tried to call someone in any level of government to get any help on anything? I am sure you have, and in most cases, I am sure they are probably still returning your call with answers to issues that no longer exist. Why! Why! Why!!! Why do these people even exist, and why does government exist except to piss you off every time or anytime you need to ask them something that is vital or important to you? Why do we bother? Live your life, and hopefully, you won't need them for anything because none of them have any COMMON SENSE or decency to call you back!! WTF do they do all day? Aren't they there to support their communities and address concerns and questions that we all have? Because these government stooges complicate every part of our lives because if they make it hard to understand, they think we need to rely on them. Don't ask, or you will get yourself blacklisted. LOL. I did have this happen to me when I tried calling my MPP a few too many times for some answers on a topic. When this MPP, which will remain nameless because, in my opinion, they are a TOOL, finally called me back to tell me they are blacklisting my email address because I emailed them too many times,

WITHOUT an answer, mind you. HOW DARE I? Asshole!!!

This is the last thing I will write about life, which I hope will resonate with all who may read this COMMON-SENSE book. The last generation that you know is slowly but now quickly leaving us for the afterlife. With this generation, which probably went through the depression, their ways, heritage, and maybe not so approved thinking with them in this now woke world, we all must learn to live in. Do yourself a favor; as the saying goes, the past always foreshadows the future. At least we forget what happened in the past, so we do not make the same mistakes in the present and in the future. That generation had a lot more common sense than any future generation will ever have, and that is because they thought things through more thoroughly than we ever will. They did things, invented things, and really cared about people. Sometimes, it didn't come across that way, but they really did. The reason I am putting this in this book is a lot of people are being blamed for past transgressions, not from the last generation but from many generations ago. Remember, one day, your generation will be judged the same way, so please use this time to be a good person and treat your fellow human beings with respect and dignity, as this will be a great reflection of the many more generations to come. Use your common sense, and ask yourself, "What would my mother say, and would my mother approve of my actions"? I will leave that with you so you can thank them before they are gone. Please say thank you to all of your grandparents and parents before it's too late for the person they helped you become.

We were going to move on to the topic of " WORK" now because it was all intertwined. But we probably will cross

16

back to life shortly once you get upset with me and the work portion I am about to discuss. Because if you think there is NO COMMON SENSE in daily life, what do you think about your work life? Because if there were, we wouldn't be asking all these questions about our fellow humans. Let's see, and I will give you some of my experiences.

2: WORK

Unless you are born into wealth or had luck winning the lottery in a big way, you will have to find your way in the working world. Even those who are born into money sometimes have to find their way, for good or for bad reasons, leaving them no option but to be part of the minions they call the working class. We all will have to do it in one form or another. This maybe for financial reasons or just to obtain some satisfaction in living life because you can't just sit on the couch and eat bon bons, or can you? lol

No matter if you work in an office, a warehouse, or at home, everyone experiences the same issues on the job. You would be surprised that we all go through the same topics and issues with work, no matter what type of work you do. You go to school, most of us do, but if you didn't and had parents that provided for you, then they all wanted one thing for their kids, and that was for them to have a better life than their parents did. Every generation has had that on their minds for generations. If they were responsible and caring parents because life is hard, and your parents, in most cases, want to make it easier for you and the next generation. The juggling of all aspects of life makes you wonder what it's all about. Don't we all ask this question some time on this journey? Why are we here? I tell ya what, it definitely isn't to schlep on the job for 40-50-60 hours a week, go home for dinner watch a little tube, and go to bed, and do it all over again, only to have the freckin' government to take over half of your hard-earned money, and then at the end of it all, "kick the bucket." Wish those morons had a little sympathy and COMMON-SENSE.

You go to school and then get a job, either out of high school or post-secondary, and you start to experience the life that everyone was preparing you for. A career they called it. You put your foot into the adult life of work. With a new job comes training and trying to learn what your responsibilities are and how to accomplish those on a daily basis. The job description you were hired to do doesn't seem to match what you are being trained for. You wonder why but are scared to ask, in fear of creating a bad first impression and getting the boss mad at you until you can figure it out on your own. Dummy, you were hired for "X," so do "X," but use some COMMON SENSE because, in the work world, there is no "X."

You went to school because most of us dreamt as kids to pursue a certain occupation as an adult. You figured out while going through grade school the requirements that are needed to meet those goals and dreams you had. So you check all the boxes, and some of you went to a trade and did well, and some of you went to a post-secondary school to obtain a degree, which was "mandatory" to get that position you dreamt about. Once you get this degree, you start to apply for that perfect job to pursue your goals and dreams. You are finally given a chance at that position and get hired by a company that can get you started.

Most companies have training to help their new people onboard and teach them how they want them to do their jobs, but why does training occur at work on a regular basis? Like the last training wasn't enough or good enough, so why was it provided, if it wasn't meant to help make things better or make changes or enhance your knowledge. Now, you are introduced to all of your work colleagues and go through all of the HR procedures put in place to cover not only you but also the company so they don't make a mistake when they hire new people. They say, "Remember you are still on probation," so you need to act a certain way. No shit, Sherlock. You are wondering if it's appropriate to ask questions until one of the other new hires starts. Boy, these questions are pretty silly, you think. Does this person have any COMMON-SENSE, you think? How the hell does he put his pants on every day? Hmm, you wonder if you are in the right job or field when this occurs. "Did I really dream as a kid to do this as a career?" you think, because it's not exactly what I thought it would be.

After the initial onboarding, you start your regular position, and you are still in the honeymoon stage of your adult work life. You meet all kinds of different people each and every day, and depending on your personality, you are either reserved or outgoing, but regardless of which type of personality you have, you start judging people and start wondering if everyone you are meeting is playing with a full deck of cards, if you know what I mean. Do any of them have any common sense from what they are saying to you? They seem to ask questions that a child would ask. Hmm, again, you wonder if you are in the right job or field. How did these people last this long here, not knowing this stuff?

You work at your position for quite some time trying to get promoted, and when you do get the occasional raise and then promotion, you wonder again if you made the right decision. " I took this promotion for peanuts, for all this stress," you say to yourself; why?? You think you know what you are doing, and then your company says you need to take some more training. We have hired an outside firm to train you on how to do your job BETTER!! Not only that but to show your team, from an outside training company, " how they can do their job better" because you really aren't doing the job that well. You think, again, we just did training with an outside firm to help us " DO OUR JOB BETTER," and now you are bringing in another firm to do what? Train us again? Did I not just get promoted so I can train my people? Huh, maybe I am the one without Common Sense? Again, am I in the right company? I wonder now. Hmm, good question. We all go through this and or went through this; if you think back at your work history, you have to smile and laugh hell ya. What a bunch of dummies we all were back then! Only if we knew then what we know now, life would be so much easier. To not take and repeat all the unnecessary, "NECESSARY" training over and over again!!LOL. Idiots without common-sense.

How many people have had training with different names but with similar objectives? WHY! WHY! WHY!. Don't we have better things to do with the 8 to 12 hours we spend at our workplace? Then, to top it off, after the full or half days of exhaustive training that is supposed to assist you in doing your job better, your company expects you to continue working, and not only that but also be productive. Do they think we do nothing during the training? They should know because they are the nuts that set it up with the discussions from the company that sold it to them. What about when you travel for work? You are on the clock 24/7. Everyone thinks it is glamorous. While it does have some perks, you are away from your family each and every day and all day, and where you need to attend meetings all day, and then at night, you need to continue to do some work and return emails or phone calls because if you don't, god forbid you to come back to an EMPTY email folder. Common sense people, please tell your managers and owners to get some or grow some and to respect your time and work, life, and balance. This is so true if these people underpay you or set unrealistic expectations of your job and position. You are actually making less than minimum wage when you travel, 24/7 on the clock. Think about it, people; use some common sense.

Why do so many companies think that everyone wants to work there? So you go through school and then possibly to post-secondary, depending on what your goals are, and then you try to figure out, " WHAT WILL MAKE YOU HAPPY?" You know that expression, do what makes you happy, and it won't feel like work. Well, while I figure that crap out, can someone please pay my freakin bills!! LOL. You want to go work somewhere or do something, and all you know is, I NEED A JOB!!. You call everyone you know to tell them you have finished school and to ask them if they know anyone who may be hiring. Everyone tells you that there are no jobs out there, and the ones that are out there are being filled only if you know someone because everyone wants to work there. What the hell are you talking about? There are more than 1 or 2 companies in this world. Why is finding a job at the beginning of your career so hard, but later on in life, it's so simple? It's like every company out there thinks you have learned so much that hiring you would bring value to their company. Have you heard of that saying, "You can't teach old dogs new tricks"? Why do companies continue to hire us old people instead of the younger ones who have an open slate and have not had their minds shaped or warped yet in the work world? I would hire a new graduate in a heartbeat over an older employee. Sorry, people in my age group. People, experience isn't always a good thing. Think about it: why does someone move companies after 15 or 20 years? Usually, there are only two reasons. First, they did something wrong or got fired because they didn't or couldn't do their job, and someone just caught on, or secondly, the company they left is probably not doing so well, probably because this person didn't do a good job, so why would you hire them?? Especially for a lateral job. Is it not a promotion? Please, people, use some COMMON sense and hire the younger kids and give them a chance. They are your future and our future, and treat them properly and correctly, especially since what has occurred over the past three years with the pandemic; more and more individuals are rethinking their goals and lifestyles and, perhaps, don't want to work for these big conglomerates any longer. Remember this, you HR people, before you hire or fire someone.

Let's move on to what happens when you actually start working at these great companies. Well, you start at the "Bottom" hoping to move up and save a bit of money, and as soon as you start, everyone tells you that you better start saving for your retirement. What the hell?? RETIREMENT, I just freakin started, so can you give me a break and let me figure this out before you want me to Retire and leave the work world. LOL. Every business or company is in existence for one purpose, and if anyone tells you otherwise, they are lying. The purpose of every single company in existence is what? We all know the truth but don't admit it. It does not provide health insurance, it does not provide a place to meet people, not a place to provide a workout facility, and definitely not a place to play video games. It's also not to promote woke activism, which we will discuss in another chapter. Businesses exist to make money and profit. Let's repeat that: MAKE MONEY, better put, make a profit for the owners that started them. If anyone tells you otherwise, again, they are lying. Companies need to make money and a profit so they can keep employing people, so these people can prop up governments with taxes and retirement withdrawals so the safety net in Canada, CPP, can be funded for the next generation. This is only for private companies, of course, because all government jobs are net takers, not net makers, as the expression goes. They are all pooch poopers when you work for the government, and it's like saying you have given up in life and want your brain cells to burn out.

After you start this new job, you try to understand what they do and why they do what they do. You start asking your colleagues questions, and if they are honest, most of the questions can't be answered, especially if the company has been around a long time. Most businesses lose their focus as to why they were started to begin with because of many reasons, but in today's world, it's because they need to be sensitive to their employees, their environment, and the world. All the precious snowflakes out there. LOL. But the ones that succeed and are respected are the ones that do and produce what they were started to do and stick to their ethics and morals. Not become subservient to the pressures of the movement of the day. Wokeness will eventually go away and die, just like Me Too and other stupid movements that produce nothing but division. You all know the movements we are talking about, the protests and marches you see on the news every day. The wokeness that we all live in nowadays. Again, more on that later, unfortunately.

So you keep asking these questions, and if you think about it, which question is the one that never really has an answer? Think about it. It's any question that you ask that starts with the word, WHY? Why is that? It's because the only person that can answer that question probably doesn't remember. Why do we do that that way? Why is pricing like that? Why do we order from these suppliers? Almost every question that was asked with the word, WHY, is answered this way.

Because we have always done it that way, if it ain't broke, why should we change? Well, genius, have you looked at what you are doing to determine if it is broken? Employees, most of the time, go through the motions each and every day until someone asks how or why they are doing what they are doing. And they say, okay, until one day they leave because things, I guess, were not okay? Why do people leave, you ask? Because you just started there and you are still in your honeymoon state, and you figure this company is great and appears to treat everyone fairly.

Then, the reality of working at a company for a period of time creeps in. Maybe these managers aren't so smart, and maybe HR doesn't care, or maybe ownership should be here more often than once a month. Hmm, did I make the right choice because time is moving on with or without you? You better make a decision if you still want to work at this company that you were sold on. Also, you better make that decision quickly, because before you know it, you will be there for 15 or 20 years, and as I said, you shouldn't be hired by another company when you get that older because you should let the younger kids have a chance. Guess what? You aren't young any longer, and life just hit you in the face!! So you go to your manager and ask how you can apply for a management job, and they look at you like, you want my job! You know what they are thinking, "You little ass, I trained you, I helped you, and this is my thanks; you want my job"? But you ask because you think that you can contribute at a more macro level to the company's success. They tell you that they will speak to HR on your behalf. Time goes by, and you don't hear anything, and then one day, they call you into their office. I had this happen to me in one of my first jobs. I came in early, I stayed late, I was a technician, making a modest wage, and they called me in after I asked about a promotion, and they said, "Sorry, but we need to let you go."? Do you think, "WTF"? You ask why, and they tell you business is slow after the company had record profits. Are you kidding me? This, I am 100% sure, has happened to everyone in the business world for one reason or another. But this is what sparks a fire in most of us. We get fired from a job we thought was what we always wanted, only to drive us to rethink our lives, and then we find something else, hopefully, better, to do, which is 1000% better and more satisfying in the long run, but does make us think as to why we wasted so much of our work life on the last company that didn't give a rat's ass about us.

You then are asked to leave all of the company technology at HR and leave the office. All the time, you are thinking, maybe what I was thinking, about either leaving or staying, manifested into me LEAVING!! And others found out? I really wanted to stay, hence the reason why I asked about being promoted. Maybe someone took that out of context, or maybe they felt that I was stepping on their feet. So here you are. You gave ten years plus to a company that basically told you that you are useless and not wanted, yet at the same time, they are hiring more people. Do they think that these new people, that they need to train, again, like they trained me, can and will do better than me? Now, you question yourself, your value, and your existence, and you walk back into the wilderness of life. I had this happen a few times in this working world of ours, as most of you probably experienced as well, until I found something I really liked to do, and I have been doing it now for 20 years. I want to thank my former employers because they showed their true colors and did me a favor. A couple of years later, one of them went out of business…HAHA, now who has the last laugh!!

Before you start looking for a NEW job, you, like all of us, start thinking about what you should do next. Maybe you should take some time off, but you hear your friends and family say, don't take too long, like I am going to forget everything I went to school for or what I learned at my last employer. If you are like most of us, not like the previous generation, who worked their entire life at one company, you look at the potential offers that have been made to you, as now you have experience and a few companies feel that you can bring some value to them and you need to pick a door, 1, 2 or 3. Please don't make that mistake again because time is running out. You have been recruited by a number of people/companies because of the skills you developed. Now, you may be able to ask for what you want, but do yourself a favor and use some COMMON-Sense because you will have to work there and need to make sure that you get that position to use as another stepping stone in the world of work. Get what you deserve, not what you think you are worth. Does that make sense, as you need to do this for another 20 or 30 years before retirement? LOL. Choose a place to work that offers you the work, life, and balance we all deserve in this world and that we all came to understand and appreciate through the pandemic. But don't take it for granted or take advantage of it!!

We all are going to go through this work life, and we need to understand why we are doing it and prioritize what is really important to each of us, or we will forget that expression I stated earlier: LIFE, WORK, BALANCE, as it's the most important phrase you need to always keep top of mind. I know a lot of people come to realize this too late, and most started to realize this during the COVID-19 pandemic, but unless you are the owner or partner of a company, you need to make sure that you don't burn out at a job. This is quite simple to do, as people take it for granted, and then, BOOM, it hits you that you have no drive or motivation any longer, and you really can't figure out why. It's not hard to get involved in your job before you realize this, so take a breath once in a while and appreciate your efforts.

I am going to share something with you from my work history. I have been in the workforce for over 40 years and have been in my current position for over 20, and I really love it. I have been in a position to report to someone and also have others report to me over the past 40 years. I remember the last two managers I worked for with whom I had many conversations. Both of them took their positions way too seriously. They thought they were splitting the atom or something. One of them got to the point of almost having a heart attack and leaving the firm because they didn't remember that phrase: work, life balance, and don't take yourself too seriously. The other was being walked over by everyone, to the point that they left the company also. No one seems to understand the phrase, a job is just a job. Unless you are the owner, even then, People, please use some COMMON-SENSE in your work-life and balance it out with your family life, and it will bring you a lot of joy.

We are all going to contribute something to society, so please make a choice that benefits you and the population in general. But please remember to be a good person along the way and show respect to everyone, even when you think they don't deserve it. We are all good people deep down!!

Now to the next topic, which is near and dear to my heart. I hate them and love them, mostly hate them, all the time. This is going to get me and you heated, so please buckle up and don't jump off the roof yet!!

3: GOVERNMENTS

How and where do you start when you talk about governments and all the people in the Western world who work for the government? This should definitely be a COMMON SENSE discussion. Really, are you freakin kidding me? How many of you have had to deal with the government, like I mentioned in the life chapter? All I can say is GOOD LUCK to you! Why do people change when they enter the government FOLD? With good or bad intentions, they always seem to change. Why?

Where is this world heading? There are many wars going on in many areas of the world, yet only one really matters, whereas millions of other people are being displaced and have been in a war for decades. Politicians are obsessed with climate change, yet the majority of the polluters don't care. The minority needs to carry the ball, and they are the ones being penalized monetarily and politically. There is a pandemic in which no one knows the origin or where it came from, and no one will take responsibility or investigate where it came from because, god forbid, we upset the world's dirtiest country! The CCCP should be condemned by the Western world and reminded why they exist. We are penalizing our kids and people who don't want to take a vaccine that apparently doesn't work, and now it has been proven it doesn't stop you from getting the virus or stop you from spreading it, yet we have politicians and their doctors, pushing for vaccines based on no or little evidence. No one really wants to address the elephant in the room except to point fingers at everyone but themselves, the people in power who can make a difference. Let's take a deep dive into a couple of these topics. But I forewarn you now, none of them will have any COMMON SENSE results associated with the topics in discussing them because we are talking about governments, the laziest and most corrupt people in parts of the Western world.

The most powerful country in the world elected a president who doesn't seem to know where he is and what day it is most of the time, yet no one wants to admit it in mainstream media. Who is really running the world's most powerful country? Does anyone really know? Everyone seems to be very happy and content that they got rid of the last one, or will they be once it's all over for this president? Everyone seems to be scared that if they say something, they will be blacklisted. No more Twitter or Facebook for you? Don't be scared, life goes on. We don't have any right to speak our minds, apparently, and if you try to voice any opinion that isn't supported by the mainstream media, you are vilified and possibly blacklisted and may lose your livelihood. How did we get here? Do we have no right to voice an opinion that isn't the mainstream opinion? And the USA VP is a piece of work. How do you get to this level in your life, and you can't string a sentence together that doesn't sound like a word salad? One of the most hypocritical politicians I have ever seen, putting away more people for simple pot possession in California but then advocating for murderers and rioters to keep going and destroying people's lives and their businesses in the USA riots of the summer of 2020. Do our southern sisters and brothers have any common sense but to vote for a couple of incompetent morons that have accomplished absolutely nothing in their political careers except to take up space and spew mainly hot useless air. I would like to watch them in a game of Scrabble and see how many dictionaries are used. Americans must really feel silly and stupid for voting for basement Joe and someone who couldn't receive more than 1% of the popular vote when she was running for the presidency. I guess there isn't a lot of common sense down there, and boy, stupid doesn't actually describe it. It's more like the wool was pulled over their heads. Let's call a spade a spade; the previous president had a lot of his own ethical issues. He was an egomaniac, but he, I believe, really cared about making change, and he tried to drain the swamp that has been built over generations, but the swamp impeached him, not once, but twice, and got away with it only fool you all in the vote of Nov 2020. And now won't leave him alone, as they are scared to death of him and that he may reveal the truth about this lifetime, scumbag bottom dwellers that pretend to be bought off politicians.

Why do politicians think that they can stay in power for 50 years or for term after term until they cant think for themselves any longer?? Why are there no term limits so we can get new blood and new thinking to lead people instead of all these corrupt individuals who would sell their own parents to get ahead and make a buck? Why are they allowed to keep running our country into the ground? You know why? Because we, the voters, let them get away with it!! How is a politician worth millions when they leave office, yet only make $150-$200k per year, yet they are worth tens of millions of dollars? Does anyone ever think to themselves, how is this possible, or do they bother asking this question? Or do they even have the time or bandwidth to think about that, as they need to feed the political beast every day with their tax dollars, which are squandered and stolen from the average taxpayer, both in Canada and the USA? They all like to waste our money on nonsense because we don't hold them accountable or ask them to put their promises in writing so we can make them resign when they all lie to us all.

Now, let's shift a bit to Canada, where we have had a drama teacher as the Prime Minister for over six years. He has criticized all types of people, and when he was caught in his past wearing blackface or doing some other questionable things he criticized others for doing, all he could do was deflect and call us all racists or names. He seems to think he is well above the average Joe in our country. He doesn't hold himself accountable, or neither do we have the ability to hold him accountable. The biggest issue in Canada is that we don't have a true democracy, and we don't vote for the Prime Minister or the Premier of the Province. We vote for one of the many minions that form the government! We should thank the UK for this monarchy rule of government!! He has written so many checks and has apologized to all types of people for historical transgressions that our great grandfathers and forefathers were involved in hundreds of years ago that we had no say in, yet he keeps doing it over and over again, and for what purpose? Who knows, and who gives a crap! Justine!! Did I just call him Justine!! Maybe that is the correct name or pronoun to use in these times. We have the Canadian government making apologies for the last 200 years of existence and the times when our forefathers ran this country. We had no say in this, but this prime minister is making false claims and writing cheques because he feels that is how you fix things instead of being honest and telling everyone, "We can't fix the past, but we can address the past atrocities moving forward and we will do better as a Country and as a people!." All he had to do was acknowledge this and move on, but he chose to write all of these taxpayer cheques instead. This idiot, and I use that word loosely, even wrote a large check to a guy who killed a US marine in wartime and who hates our country and then apologized to him on behalf of Canadians. This guy should hang somewhere and go"f" himself with our $10 million. Well, let me tell you, PM, did you ask me if I wanted to apologize to a murderer? Or anyone of the hardworking Canadians that definitely don't give a crap. He paid this asshole $10 million, yes, $10 million, and said sorry, we were wrong. Are you freaking kidding me, Justine!!! What gives this jackass the right to send my hard-earned tax dollars to a killer. He doesn't even have a MAJORITY government and has no right to do this, but no one holds him accountable. Do you know why? Because none of these jerks have any COMMON SENSE. And any balls to tell him to go pound salt. Our PM should be put on trial for abuse of the public purse if there is such a law, as he would be convicted, in my opinion, many times over for his nonsense and all of these apologies and checks he has written!!

You know the Trudeaus always get kickbacks, but god forbid you say anything because PET was the immigrant's perfect PM. A number of their friends have given them free all-expenses-paid trips, kickbacks like the WE charity scandal, and all the "free" vacations, and no one is ever held accountable or put in jail. It all must be a coincidence that all of these freebies just show up for these Trudeaus?? And when they are caught, all they do is say "sorry." we didn't think it was against the law or morals or non-ethical. Really Jackass!! "We will pay it back, not from my pocket but the taxpayer can pay for this and accept the bill because I can!" Why don't you try to get a kickback from a charity and tell me how much jail time you will get? Or how the CRA would hold you accountable. Why doesn't anyone in government get charged and put in jail for doing these things that are illegal? We have a number of MPs and MPPs involved in these types of scandals each and every year, and never does anyone ever get charged or made to pay any reparations.

Again, all they do is say " Sorry" for getting caught. Some may feel guilty and resign, only to run for political office in the future and win because we have short memories here of being screwed over! This is no democracy, and there is no equal justice for all, but one set of policies and rules for us taxpayer folks and one for the ingrate politicians who all think they are above the law!

Here is a very volatile topic for a number of people and for a number of reasons. We live in a country that has a leader that we never voted for, as I stated earlier. Since when does a democracy exist where you don't get a vote for the leader? We are governed by what they say is the British parliamentary system because we are part of the Commonwealth and under the Queen, and now under the King. It appears, in Canada, we are slaves to the master, who is the PM, because the PM does whatever the PM wants to do with no accountability, and when the PM wants to take more of the slave's money, they do, such as the CARBON TAX, that doesn't go to fight CARBON, but goes into GENERAL revenues!! And you nor I can do anything about it, since they have a Majority, or sorry, they don't have a Majority, but a Minority government, yet they act like they have a Majority being propped up by a bunch of other clown politicians called the NDP!

So when is democracy, not a democratic process? When you can vote, but not vote for the leader of the Country or for your province. Doesn't anyone ever ask that question? How come you can't vote for the leader, yet they make all the decisions based on a majority government or maybe a minority government that is propped up by a bunch of idiots? I am sure if you sit down and think about this, it will start to upset you. The leader puts together policy with input from the cabinet, supposedly, but your member of parliament, be it an MP or MPP, never seems to be in that cabinet, even though they got elected. How is that democratic? Think of the word DEMOCRATIC. Demo means devil in Latin and God in Greek, and Cratic is associated with strength. What is democracy if you are not involved, and when you are, it doesn't really matter? Perfect example, the government you didn't vote for passes a new tax, CARBON TAX, let's say, and can't tell you why and where the money is going, yet tells you it's best for all of us. You think it's not good for me, so don't blow smoke up my pipe because you are so self-absorbed and couldn't put that question in a referendum format for true democracy to work. You were not voted in to take more of our Money. You promise to make Canada carbon neutral, which, believe me, is not possible unless you take all the cars off the road and close all of the companies in this country that use any fossil fuel-generated energy. You know what you have then, a desert of a country that wouldn't exist. So they are ALL lying to us, and none of them can be held accountable because we didn't vote for them, and they don't have a majority to pass this type of legislation, and if they try to, they should put it into a referendum, and then they will see what the true feelings of the population really is. They will be very surprised. Do you know why? BECAUSE THE MAJORITY OF PEOPLE DO HAVE COMMON SENSE. Not like all these idiots that don't live in the real world but in their idealist world wearing rose-colored glasses. Why they always chose to tell us half-truths is quite interesting instead of telling us the whole story so we can make an informed decision. If only they did what they were put into their positions to do, which is to make this country and their citizens a better life for all and create prosperity for all. These governments all do one thing well, and that is to lie as often as possible so as to confuse the population and then point fingers, as they do, and blame others, such as grocery stores, for inflation, instead of holding themselves accountable. Canada was a great country, and then we voted in another TRUDEAU!! When will we learn?

When is the last time a politician made a promise during their election or re-election, in most cases, to do, wait a minute, LOWER YOUR TAXES? Or even better, keep the promise they made? Have you ever heard a politician say that? I do mean, LOWER your taxes or STOP any future tax increases? Think about it for a minute because if you are reading this, you are probably pissed off and have voted a number of times, and have been paying personal taxes, consumption taxes, and property taxes for quite some time as one small example of a tax you pay if you have the privilege of owning? Think about that phrase: LOWER YOUR TAXES!! Never has this ever happened, and if it has, they probably lied and/or put a caveat to it, like, if I can, or if it's doable or wait for it,' IT'S A STRETCH GOAL.' Have you heard that one somewhere? Remember that piece of work and her stretch-exaggerating goals? No, why don't you make a promise like that? Because if you do, all of the government workers, who are mainly unionized, would lose their minds. Why don't you ask your politician in the next election to make that promise and put it in writing? And if they get elected and don't follow through, ask them to put it in writing that they will resign because they lied to you. Remember, it's your money, and the people with Common sense should hold all of these goofballs accountable as to how they spend out hard-earned dollars that they steal from us each and every day until we die. They keep raising these taxes each and every year to waste on stupid. Non-sensical ideas that they feel are worthy! So they can pay all their government buddies bonuses each and every year with no real goals and keep giving all of these lazy-ass government workers crazy raises, benefits, and pensions that the majority of private employees will never get!

All you hear from all of these lifetime politicians is vote for us because we will do this or that with your money. We will spend it here, and spend it there, and help all of the underprivileged who don't have as much as you. We will expand our social safety nets that YOU will never use! We will provide more services and opportunities for them and will try to make everything EQUITABLE. What the F is Equitable? We are in the www. World. Stages in life and all possible services that can be thought of have been provided, so how can you possibly provide any more services or delivery anything more than we already have in this over-taxed country called Canada? Well, they can't, and all they are doing is trying to appease their own shortcomings. They want to provide everything to all and be all to everyone, and we all know that any political idea is not worth the paper it is written on, is it? Has any politician ever thought of a way to do more with less, just like the private sector is asked to do, year in and year out? Do they even know what that means? Have they ever had to do with less themselves? Maybe on the odd occasion, but that is rare because once you are in politics, it appears you remain in politics for the remainder of your adult life. And they go on, and they seem to forget why they got into politics to begin with, which is to serve the greater good. But, I don't think any of them have ever thought of that, and all they really thought of was the end game of larger paychecks, all the perks, and the brown paper envelopes that they would be receiving when they cater to the greed that they see and they contribute to. Don't forget those gold-plated pensions that they all dream of. 10-1 PAYMENTS: this is incredible. We all pay for this craziness for people who are no smarter than you or me! Are they really? Think about it. Who or what are politicians, and what makes them a politician? They are either born into that world or think they can make a difference and enter that world only to become part of the swamp!

How can we elect people who have traits that we all agree with? We all don't have the same goals in life, but we all should have common sense and should be able to agree on mutually agreeable topics. We can also agree to disagree, as the saying goes. But, one thing we all should have in common IS common sense, and we should NOT act like we are stupid, especially if someone is running for political office. You would think these people would be oozing common sense, but maybe we are all naïve. Maybe we are the ones that are having the wool being pulled over our eyes. They all seem to get into politics to gain power, fortune, and future political positions when people get tired of them eventually and vote them out. Think of all the former politicians, in Canada specifically, both Federally and Provincially, that were in your district and what they are doing now. I bet, if you look them up, they are probably working in some political appointment, a government agency, or an educational institution, which are usually owed or paid for in some form by the taxpayer. How and why do these USELESS people always seem to move on to a prestigious position within some public organization? Or here is the bigger one: they get appointed to either some large company board of directors or hired as a VP within some large corporations that they probably lobbied for in one form or another while they were in government and changed or influenced change in some sort of legislation. And if you dig deeper, you can probably, in most cases, find some sort of affiliation to this company, that they passed some sort of law or bylaw of some kind to benefit these companies. Why do all of these former politicians land on their feet and keep running while most people who lose their jobs go through a tough time finding another position? How about the politicians that hold a political office of some sort and, while holding that office, run for another higher political office without resigning their current post, just in case they don't win the new election? How is this even possible? Are we all stupid for not holding any of them accountable, or are we the only ones in this world that do the right thing all of the time? Or how about the politicians, who are paid severance when they lose their election? This happens in many towns and cities, where the loser gets paid a severance package because they lost the election. Have you heard of anything more STUPID, and that really doesn't make sense? You run for a political office, get elected, and are supposed to contribute to your local community and then get paid even more when you lose because you are doing a shitty job. Who the hell can make any COMMON SENSE out of this? Who gets severance when you are voted out of office? This isn't a typical 9-5 job; it's an elected official who isn't held accountable for anything they do, except when it's time for re-election. These people barely work a couple of hours a week; if we are lucky, that is when they are not at a photo opp to benefit themselves. And then viola, they lose, cry, complain, and then they get severance? Then, get a political appointment and move on because they were useless in what they did or didn't do, and that's why they probably didn't get re-elected!! Have you ever thought of running for office, or do you have too many scruples and morals and think you couldn't do what they do, but you probably could, and you probably could do it even better because you would always have the best interest of your constituents in the forefront. You will spend taxpayers' money responsibly; wouldn't that be a change to these no-common-sense idiots? Why would they choose to spend your tax money responsibly? Wow!

Enough with Stupid politicians that don't have any common sense because we could all write about these morons for a long time, a very long time. Why do they exist, and how do you think they sleep at night knowing that they squandered your hard-earned dollars, which they keep stealing from you and keep spending on stupid pet projects that will never benefit anyone except a few people in their own riding or community or maybe even personally in one form or another! Hmm, isn't that interesting?

We have governments that award million or billion-dollar tenders with limited competition, that are not held accountable for projects that run massively over budget and well over completion dates, and again, no one is ever fired or held to pay anything back, and all they do is say "SORRY". Can you say Metrolinx for those people who live in Ontario?

Let's move on to why governments were invented and made to exist. They were created so they can give us all direction and put in laws that have checks and balances so we all live in a very humane society that protects us all and gives us all some safety nets and the ability to prosper in society. Isn't that the purpose of government in North America, specifically in Canada, is to provide a systematic way for the majority of its citizens to enjoy a safe and prosperous life, and when stuff happens, the citizens can rely on some social safety nets?

Governments go way back in time. When some people wanted to reserve power over other people, this was usually done and achieved by some sort of war or fighting that caused fear and apprehension. Governments first came to fruition as people discovered that protection was easier if they stayed together in groups and if they all agreed that they had some common interests in that group; hence, they coerced many people to join that same group and lead them all as a unit. Or maybe this was called the Mafia, LOL! They were supposed to serve the group that they gathered as one until they realized that they could do a lot more, and they didn't need the consensus of the entire group to do whatever they wanted to and whatever was self-serving. That is called a majority, not a minority, geniuses. I think this is also referred to as a gang mentality or, as stated, the Mafia. Isnt it? They all seem to forget why they were created or voted into power, and that was to serve the larger power of the group that formed them. Then they evolved, or we should say, morphed, into something they couldn't control or couldn't be held accountable to or for. It appeared that Common Sense was thrown out the window because the powers in charge realized they could do anything at any time because they thought they were voted into power without any ramifications or accountability. To this day, nothing has really changed regarding government or its powers, except they have become bigger, stronger, more powerful and have been truly arrogant, and think they can do anything, at any time, to anyone, with, again, no accountability or ramifications, because the swamp protects itself and its creatures in it. They get into politics and stay in politics; the majority do until they either get caught with something or they realize they can't look themselves in the mirror any longer and continue to do what they do, which is usually unconscionable. Use some of their GOD-given common-sense brains. Or not!

I am writing this to bring to life that Common sense still exists, I think, but maybe there is a range of Common sense or what is perceived to be common sense. You voted for someone, and they think, from a common sense perspective, they can do everything and anything and not be held accountable. What makes a politician think they have the tools, rights, or experience to do anything but what they were voted to do.? Governments should try to make things less onerous for their constituents and citizens and less expensive, where possible for them as well. They keep raising fees and taxes because they think they can. And how about some of these higher position politicians that are appointed to specific roles, let's say, a Minister of Foreign affairs? This is a very high-profile role that interacts with other nations and government entities. They make all these promises on behalf of the country they represent, but forgetting one very important point: they were not given a mandate, and in this case, to propagate war and fund a war because they didn't ask their people if they wanted to fund a war. Who in their right mind, living in the first world, would want to fund a war that has nothing to do with your country? And what gives this individual, or this government, especially if they were not given a majority government, the right to prop up a country that is probably the most corrupt in this world and doesn't want to sit down and negotiate a settlement? Yes, I am speaking of Ukraine, which should look in the mirror before asking others for help! One of the most corrupt countries in this entire world who keeps asking for help and provides no help to their own cause. Who has any common sense in the year 2022 and believes war is going to solve anything except kill innocent people and uproot their citizens.? Maybe all of these refugees can come to North America to live a more free life away from corruption and war? Governments, especially peacekeeping ones like Canada, should never, ever fund a war that doesn't directly affect them. Disputes, and in this case a war, solve nothing, as I stated, and they should be fought if needed amongst the combatants, and not involve other parties that have no vested interest, no matter what a lying politician may tell you. It will continue, this one, the next one, and so on, and each and every one of them will be propagated by a lying politician. No matter what a lying politician tells you, they will never tell you the truth. War is not an option for anything as far as I am concerned, especially if it doesn't really affect you or your country directly. There is no purpose to war in this time and age, no matter what anyone says. Wars are only started for power and to gain that power over other people and countries, as it was in the past, but for some reason, no one nowadays remembers the past in this realm, as this is what should be remembered and never forgotten from history. War solves nothing!! It only makes companies and corrupt people- and corrupt countries very rich. Hence, the reason wars are started and maintained for long periods of time is for purposes of generating power and money for corrupt regimes, people, and politicians.! A lot of people, companies, and countries become really rich off of their tax base because of wars!

We have problems in this country and severe ones that this government, no matter which one is in power, refuses to address. Now, we can move on to financially supporting a war no one understands or agrees with.

Why are governments, especially the Western world, USA, and Canada, obsessed with spending billions and billions of dollars of taxpayers' money on a war that means absolutely nothing to most people? It's a war between a couple of countries that are both corrupt, so who cares? Let them kill each other if they want, as a number of other wars in this world have been ongoing for years, if not decades and no one in the western world has ever addressed, except this one, why? Why is this war more important to anyone except the two countries involved? And why does one of the countries, the Ukraine, keep asking the Western world and every other democratic country to keep supplying weapons and money? Billions and billions of dollars, but no one ever asks where this money is going. Now we kind of know that some, if not a lot, is being embezzled by corrupt politicians. There is no accountability for all of this money from the countries providing the help or the country receiving all of these billions of dollars. Why and why are taxpayers tolerating this freakin craziness? Ukraine is the world's leader in the export of wheat grains and fertilizer, yet they have no money to defend their citizens. Has anyone asked them where all of their money from these exports is or has gone? Or are they just corrupt like most governments are in the western world that keep stealing this from their citizens and expropriate this money for other things, and stupid pet projects that bring zero value to any taxpayer? Should we just say the money is stolen by these corrupt politicians? Where is the Ukraine's money, and why doesn't anyone ask this question? Their economy was doing well, so where did all of their money go? Ask your politician next time they call you for your vote. These are the same leaders that are posing for front covers of global magazines while their people are being killed. What kind of freakin priorities are those? I want to be on the front cover while you soldiers can go to the front of the war. Idiots, all of them, idiots without COMMON SENSE. They keep fighting for something, but never tell anyone what that something is, but they want to call it democracy. By the way, Ukraine is not a democracy in my opinion? Look it up!

I am going to turn back to the subject of accountability for all levels of our government. Governments keep creating these NGOs, and I will give you a perfect example in Ontario. They created something called Metrolinx in 2006 to coordinate mass transit and projects in that field, such as buses and subways. This organization started with only a handful of people but has morphed into a goliath and handles most if not all, the transportation projects in Ontario. The reason I bring this up is this organization is a perfect example of waste with no accountability. They keep starting useless projects that contribute ZERO to better your life, yet they keep going and growing.

They developed bus projects in a lot of jurisdictions ranging from Toronto, Newmarket, and Markham, where they ripped up miles and miles of road to put the bus lanes in the middle of 4 or 6 lanes roads and then created such a backlog on these roads, that no one seems to understand how much these type of bus projects have contributed to congestion with the perception they are helping the greater good. Metrolinx thinks that by expediting buses they are negating carbon emissions without realizing very few people take these buses, which cause cars to idle even longer, negating any positive effect they may think they have and negate the carbon offsets with all of theses cars excessive idling. They created advanced bus turn lanes that keep people idling their cars for longer periods, contributing more to the previous topic of climate change. They spent billions and billions of dollars on each project, and all they did was create more traffic with these advance lights for buses that may hold 10-

15 people at a time. These projects will never make back a portion of the costs, with ZERO ROI, but these people who are paid quite well don't seem to really care. There is no accountability of COMMON-SENSE. The CEO of this organization is paid a lot of money and held to ZERO accountability. Why has no one asked this CEO for an ROI on these projects? You know why, because perception is better than reality in life sometimes, when you are a politician, that accomplishes absolutely nothing during their term except waste time money! Other peoples money that is!!

Then there is the Toronto Subway extension they were in charge of, which has destroyed lives and people's businesses. The project came to light that there was no real completion date or price tag that vendors need to abide by. The price tag went from around $6 billion to over double that, with, as I stated, no reasonable completion date. When they were asked, no one at Metrolinx gave any answers or statements because, in my opinion, there are a lot of kickbacks and corruption in the bid that was awarded for this once-in-a-generation project. How is it possible that people and companies, agencies, or governments can do what they do without any accountability and keep squandering our money and then, when they are confronted, hide behind red tape and excuses? This is the world we live in Big government and big corruption. - no common sense and/or accountability. They all seem to be crooks without the experience to manage anything except wasting taxpayer money. I don't quite understand why we tolerate these bunch of idiots. They should all go to jail, in my opinion, because when you cant answer a simple question, you are either lying or hiding something much bigger, such as corruption!

We have all levels of governments asking their citizens to pay more and more and never being held accountable for any of their actions, good or bad, mainly bad, because they feel entitled. What gets into a politician's head to think they are above the law and want more? There is a mayor in the city of Toronto who is complaining they have a budget deficit of over $800 million, blames it all on COVID-19, and begs each level of government to contribute to closing this gap, but no one wants to ask the hard questions. Why is there such a large deficit? Where did it come from? Was it Covid? If so, what did you do, Mr Mayor, regarding your budget during Covid? Did you lay anyone off from your over 50,000 city employees/contractors? Did you lower the service of your transit system, which only had a 10% ridership, or did you keep paying everyone their full pay and benefits with no accountability? What did you do to lower your spending? Do you know how many of those questions were asked of this mayor? Wait for this, NONE, because no one has the balls to do so? Or the COMMON-SENSE to do so, because god forbid they offend the privileged. We ALL have to pay more because of politicians who don't know how to balance a checkbook or have any sense of morality. How can someone run their household this way without going bankrupt? Well they cant, but government can because they can always print money and keep stealing more from the taxpayer!

Since when is a politician an expert in any subject, topic, or field? Look at the current PM in Canada who has never balanced a checkbook, and his favorite saying is, "Budgets will balance themselves"—a perfect couple of examples when some are appointed to cabinet posts. The finance minister can't balance a checkbook, in my opinion, because they used to be a journalist. A defense minister never wore a uniform, yet they seem to think they can send billions of dollars to an endless war without asking them for any accountability or forecasts or peace talks? Ask them when was the last time they picked up a gun or negotiated a peace treaty. Then there is the foreign affairs minister, who has never been out of the country but appointed to represent the country all over the world. These are all fictitious but somewhat true examples of political appointments without real-life experience running our world all over the world. And you wonder what the F, is wrong with this picture. All these individuals seem to believe they possess superior knowledge, yet they consistently shroud themselves in secrecy, refraining from providing reasons or responding to direct inquiries but expect us to keep paying, and they keep stealing from us to fund their non-sensical wars and corrupt projects. I will probably have repeated some of this, but why do these people want to fund one stupid war, Ukraine, but none of the other ones that have been proliferating in this world for decades? Ask them this question when a war starts the next time and they don't want to fund it? Never mind the next one, where ever that maybe, and you better believe another one is just around the corner, so it can distract the taxpayer in another way, and make them feel bad that they are living a better life than a war torn country, so more money can be wasted and sent to countries that are corrupt!

Common-sense needs to exist, especially in governments, for us all to have a chance at a better life in this world, but it never will until these people are held accountable, and this will never be done by elections in Canada, especially because you can never vote for any leaders, or any issues, because they will never put the issues on a referendum or ballet. The only way that they can be held accountable is if we all decide not to pay any more taxes. Yes, you heard me. What if you try to start a petition in your small town or city and get everyone in that town to agree not to pay another single dollar of property tax? What do you think that mayor would or could do? Will they expropriate all of the town's homes, or will they maybe think twice, when they can't pay their employees and give them crazy raises, benefits, or pensions moving forward? Maybe someone should start this revolt and see what happens. Hmm, isn't that an interesting question or thought? Wish I was a lawyer so I could defend everyone for free to try this one time, Don't you? I am sure you have thought about it: why are we paying property taxes, especially when you bought the house, and now it is turning into a rental because of your tax bill? Hmm. There is never enough taxes to be paid in the western world by the taxpayer property tax, employment tax, consumption tax, and maybe even carbon tax, that does absolutely nothing. There is NEVER enough. Why is that?

Do you ever wonder why governments, all of them, feel entitled? Why do all their employees feel that way also? Its as if someone gave them all a book on Power once they get a job with the government. They feel like they can act differently or talk down to you and maybe go on those power trips. Think about the last time you called your MP or MPP or any politician for that matter, or tried crossing the border and interacting with a CBSA officer. How did they speak to you? What was the demeanor? Did you get that feeling the were better than you and looked down at you as their training manuals probably told them to do? Do any of these people have any COMMON-SENSE, you wonder? Do they realize that you are the one who pays their salaries, benefits, and pensions? Probably not!! Most of these people act like jerks. Why is it governments feel entitled, as I stated earlier, and feel they can keep taking from you instead of trying to work within a balanced budget like you have to do each and every day in your life? Why do they think they can keep stealing our money and creating a huge deficit on the government credit card that eventually will have to be paid? Governments are NET TAKERS, not NET MAKERS, as the expression goes, but they think they are doing us all a favor. Maybe one day, the average person or citizen will be given a voice in our society to put these people in their place. Maybe one day, someone with money will take the government to the Supreme Court to stop the STEAL I am referring to because sooner or later, the private sector, which pays for the public sector, will not only run out of tax money but they will also run out of patience. Governments need to look in the mirror and stop and work within their means like we all do. Use some common sense because people will not pay 10k or 12k a year in property taxes because that is where we are heading. It will be cheaper to be a renter and not an owner, as I mentioned previously, and then not a taxpayer. Governments better start taking sight of this overreach because it will come back to bite them in the ass sooner or later. I hope its sooner, because a lot of people's patience is truly running out! Ask your neighbor what's on their mind, and I don't think you would be surprised. They will probably tell you what they are thinking; "I am tired of all of these taxes"!!

Common – Sense will prevail, but it will be too late for all governments around the world when it does!! Politicians need to stop acting like overseers and start acting like the employees they are, because they work for you and me, and they all need to answer the hard questions! Keep asking them the hard ones and they may actually tell you the truth!! Don't hold your breath!!

In Canada, we have three levels of government: Municipal, Provincial and Federal. Have you noticed non of these goofs, can ever balance a budget or say no to a special interest group or project, that means nothing. No of these levels has any common-sense ideas or views like the common folk. Have you also noticed, that the most important levels, Feds and Province, that you can't vote for the leader of the party. Why is that? What type of democracy do we have, where we cant vote for the leader. Maybe one day, they will realize, as I stated earlier, they work for you and me, and don't run their own money losing businesses trying to appease the entire world!! Common-sense people, you were given some, please try using a little of it!!

Let's hold these people accountable moving forward, everyone because that's the only way out of this entire mess we in the western world call DEMOCRACY! There is a lot more that can be written about this topic, but it will never end because all that governments do is frustrate most, if not all, of their citizens.

Let's now move on to how they steal our money under the disguise of the word TAXES! This topic, of taxes, will probably effect you so negatively if you haven't thought about how much you actually pay, each and every year, and that figure seems to be growing, each and every year. Good Luck!

4: TAXES

Common-sense doesn't work in the world of Taxes either. I believe the word taxes should be an oxymoron because it contradicts everything we work and stands for, in my opinion. Again, no one has any common sense because taxes were implemented and needed due to the world war, so we were tricked to believe, and they were only supposed to be temporary, but most people are not old enough to remember this. Or they choose not to do any historical research to understand why they are being fleeced for more than 50% of their earnings each and every year. Here we go. Have an open mind and then get a little pissed off. You should while I review this topic, which isn't very popular unless you don't work or are a lefty and socially dependant. Let's have a candid discussion about taxation, the level of taxation, the evil need for it, and the pain it causes a lot of people, especially in the western hemisphere.

Why do you work 40, 50, or 80 hours a week and then give 40-50% of your money to the government? Has anyone every told you why they need any of your money, not to mention almost 50% of it on a regular basis? What do you get for that money? They keep saying things like free health care, support services, clean drinking water, policing, and the best one is "for a social safety net" for everyone. You think, why the hell do I care about a social safety net for everyone? You have worked from a young age and have never collected anything through this so-called "social safety net," so why the hell are you paying for it? Don't get me started on the "FREE HEALTH CARE" we receive. When have you ever heard, "Nothing in life is Free," so why are we told our Health Care is "Free?" I guess you get what you pay for; if it's free, you better count on waiting a long time to get it. When was the last time you got this free health care? How long did you need to wait, or were you referred by your Family MD if you are lucky enough to have one, and then the "Specialist" mails you an appointment for 6-12 months from today? Wow, thanks; I can cross the border, pay $500, and get the same or better service the same day!! Frustrating or what? So, all of these "FREE" services that your taxes pay for, are you taking full advantage of them? I bet you are not because you are freakin too busy working to pay for all of these "FREE" services. Why don't they just take 20-25% of my money for these "FREE" services, and then maybe I might be okay with that?

Remember how much tax you pay. Income tax, property tax, gas tax, consumption tax, all the way upto 18% if you are lucky to live in one of those lucky provinces and wait for this, the CARBON TAX, so Canada, the most conservation and socially responsible country in the world doesn't even pollute, except if you are privileged enough to fly on the Prime Minister plane around the world! How you ever added up how much you pay each year? Well, I did, and I pay well over 60% each year, because I get free heath care and a social safety net. Thanks, Justin, and Doug!

Speaking about crossing the border, have you ever crossed the border for the day, if you are close to one, and bought a couple of things, maybe $100 worth, and then you need to pay taxes on it when you come back? The CBSA agent will ask you, "Anything to Declare?" God forbid if you don't say, "Yes." They may very well fine you even more. Is this frustrating? And have you ever wondered why you can't spend your AFTERTAX dollars anywhere you want? Why does your government make you pay duties on aftertax dollars? Don't they steal enough from us already!! That really pisses me off. They take, like I said, about 50% from your paycheck without even asking, and then you still want to pay GST, HST, Gas Tax, and as much as they want, and whenever they want. I only wanted to cross the border to buy some items that may not even be available in Canada due to the limitations and the stubbornness of this great government. We have – BOOM - sorry, sir, but you owe another 13% on your purchase. Huh, why? I know for a fact the border agents can't or won't even answer that question because I think they are all trained to act like a typical government or insurance company only, deny, distract, or redirect the question. So, please go spend your money where you get the most bang for it and use the COMMON – SENSE the LORD gave you, or you will not make it through this part of your life - the tax-sucking government part. You paid tax on that item you purchased in the USA, so why do you need to pay more? Don't we have a USMCA agreement with them and doesn't it cover me!! LOL.

Have you ever wondered why the Canadian government has such a large CRA department? There are thousands of auditors that work for the CRA who will scrutinize your tax return. God forbid you submitted an honest tax return, so you cross your fingers that you don't receive an email or a letter in the mail like I did asking for additional information. They take, from me anyway, and most of us, about 40% or so at source, if you want to live any type of life in Canada. Again, most people work 40-50 hours a week to just survive and feed the beast we call the government. Then they say, sorry, but you need to send us some more information about the claims you made in your tax return. You look at the letter, in my case, and they want doctor's information for my disabled child, whom they, the government diagnosed, themselves and whom I claimed as a dependant. They want me to send them copies of all the doctor's receipts to prove that they are legitimate fees and charges that I paid, with aftertax dollars, to show them that my kid is truly disabled and needs these services that I paid for, even though we have FREE healthcare. Is this COMMON-SENSE in your mind because, unless I am missing something, like a couple of screws in my head, it definitely isn't, and most of these government people and agencies that we fund with our tax dollars should be shrunk and minimized because they are not necessary, only a vast waste of time and money? Think about what I just said: they want more proof that my kid is disabled, even though they diagnosed him?

At one time back in the 90's, one of the smartest ideas was presented by a MP, who wanted to implement a single tax for everyone in Canada. I believe it was 20-25% for everyone. The form was a single page, and no one would receive any writeoffs. Imagine that, everyone, if you make $1 or a $1 billion would pay the same, and I think that was brilliant. The only problem with it, was each level of government would need to cut their tax collects by 70% and god forbid, we use our money effectively, and not waste it on paper pusher and gold-plated pension for all of these entitled people. Again, best idea anyone has ever present that feel on deaf ears! No need for GST, HST or any other government tax, as everyone would pay, no matter your situation. Fair and Common-sense idea!

My specific tax case was simple compared to some of my friends, who run their own businesses and pay through the teeth, as it is called, and then they get audited because this expense or that expense got put in the wrong column. I have two friends that this happened to, and both are straight-up business owners. And both had to spend thousands, and I mean thousands of dollars, hiring lawyers to fight the accusations from revenue Canada and the CRA, while these clowns have already taken 100's of thousands of tax dollars from them for a couple of extra bucks. Imagine having to hire a lawyer to fight tax law because the government feels you didn't pay enough or tried to submit an expense that they didn't agree with. Where the F do we live? In a 3rd world country, obviously, or they wouldn't be so arrogant with us taxpaying citizens. Pay your taxes, shut up, or we will make your life a living hell. Sure, that takes a lot of COMMON SENSE, doesn't it? We are all stupid to tolerate this nonsense. All these government agencies waste our tax dollars and are not held accountable for anything, but we, the taxpayers, need to be scrutinized for EVERYTHING!! Common people, use your Common-Sense. Stop screwing us, and live within your means like we taxpayers need to do each and every day! You bunch of morons!

Now, they implemented a carbon tax that goes nowhere because Canada is probably the smallest contributor to "CLIMATE CHANGE," a term I use very, and I do mean very, loosely, in the G7. More about this scam and the consternation it is causing us Canadian taxpayers below! But this is the stupidest thing I have ever heard. Collect tax money to plant some trees, buy some "CARBON CREDITS," another loosely used term, and while all of these government goofballs travel on government planes with 30-50 people to visit all of these countries for all of these summits, G7, G20 and all of these other silly G meeting, to talk nonsense and what they can do to impact this so-called: CLIMATE CHANGE? Are they the only part of the civilization, the government and its workers, that haven't heard of ZOOM or TEAM's technology? FYI, idiots, no carbon emissions emitted or no Carbon credits are needed to use those two platforms. Oh, but I regressed and forgot about not being able to expense food and drinks on the taxpayers' dime. Oh, forgot, that's yours and my dime. They don't give a rat's ass about you or me. All these jackasses care about is themselves and their perception of the life they want to lead, regardless of how it affects this so-called climate change? They all travel to these places, just like in 2022, to Cambodia and then Thailand, for a G20 summit because none of these asses have ever heard of ZOOM or TEAMS. Again, then they have the hypocritical nerve to scold us for maybe using our gas cars to go to work to pay them the taxes they need, so they can act like gods and judges, not like the elected officials that they should act like. I guess they forget why they got elected in the first place. One day, they will learn!! But it will be too late for the taxpayers that are being fleeced. Because they all know better than the hard-working taxpayer!! Idiots, all of them!! Now, on April 1, 2023, the Canadian government increased the carbon tax from $50/ton to $65/ton and didn't give a rat's ass as to tell us how it affects everyday Joe. Let's see, that's at least 3 cents for each litre of car gas, another increase in your natural gas monthly bill from Enbridge, another monopoly in Ontario, and let's not count all the increases in everything you buy from your grocery store and other purchases you make. Do you really understand why we have inflation? Its because of all of these taxes. Even the BANK OF CANADA governor stated that they cant get inflation to the level they want, because of all the excessive government spending! Go figure geniuses, NO COMMON-SENSE, you cant keep spending and printing money and then say, its expensive! Oh, but wait, the Canadian government will send you back a couple of bucks per family as a carbon credit so you can pay for some of those increased costs!! Common-sense people, because stealing another dollar from us and then giving us back 10 cents is pretty sneaking and evil!! So you may pay a couple thousand dollars more per year to save the planet, yea right, and the Canadian government may send you back a couple hundred of you tax dollars they stole from you for another brilliant idea!!

From Income tax, property tax, and consumption tax, when does it stop? Why do we pay so much? You go to work, and you make $1000/week, but you put $600 in the bank, and you try to find out why. Why do you work so hard and can never get ahead? Wow, you were always told by your parents, "Just work hard, and you will succeed." Well, Mom and Dad, I have been working hard, 50 hours a week, and I owe more than I have, and I look around, and there are people that don't work and are doing better than I am". Doesn't that just upset you to the point you have no words to describe it!! You just want to scream at these government morons. The net takers keep taking and increasing the take, each and every year, from the net makers. Boy, this is so frustrating, but again non of these asses give one iota of crap, as long as we pay for everything and fund their gold-plated pensions!!! Common-sense tells me to go vote for someone that cares! Oh, I forgot the ones that do, don't want that crappy job!! When will this insanity stop? Has anyone ever thought of spending less from a government perspective! Are you joking! You can always get more blood from a stone, as one genius government employee stated. LOL. All of these workers, have no COMMON-SENSE, because when the horse leave this barn the gravey train will be gone!

So you make a decision and save enough to buy a house, but did you ever think of the costs of home ownership, especially all of the extra fees and property taxes? Well, I have owned a few homes, and in my present home, my water bill has gone up 200% and my property taxes about 70% in the past 14 years, and now my heating and electric bills have also increased by 30 to 40% without explanation. You all know what I mean. You are experiencing the same thing, look at your Enbridge bill, your Rogers bill, and your electricity bill. They are all going up. Everything is going up, except your net take home pay check. LOL

Everyone thinks we are all making a million dollars per year and keep raising everything. All levels of governments, all of this corporations and anyone that thinks they can ask for more from the taxpayer. They all keep us oppressed by taking more from us and not providing any value or return to us, the taxpayer.

Hmm, maybe I am getting more services for these fees, or maybe the town needs more money. What the hell do I care, except that I keep paying more and not getting anymore in terms of services or value? Small or large governments don't have any accountability for what they do and how they spend our HARD-EARNED after-tax dollars. Why do they need property taxes when we pay all of those income taxes that are supposed to be shared equally? Have you ever thought about that or asked yourself that question? There is only one taxpayer that funds every level of government, municipal, provincial, and federal, but they all act like there is more than one taxpayer with unlimited funds!! They will find out sooner or later that this Ponzi scheme is unsustainable when all the cards come crashing down!! Governments were setup for a few reasons, and most of these reasons were for basic needs, such as maintaining roads, offering policing, garbage pickup and clean water, but now every level of government seems to want to be everything to all people, with all of thes non-sensical ideas and projects they think they need to fund! Well stop it you idiots, we don't need you for anything but the basics, and that's even a stretch!

I will give you an example of how these stupid people spend our money, the money of people with Common senses. Well, are you waiting? In my town, we used to flood the local park in the winter to make it a skating rink for all of the residents of the town. This happened in multiple parks in town. Each morning or evening, a machine would push off all the snow if needed, and the rink would be good to go for all the kids and wanna-be pro players who are reliving their youth. They flood the park a little every other day. Well, that went on for many, many years. Then, all of a sudden, the town decides to buy a very expensive, and I mean, very expensive, portable ice rink that takes ten or so people to build each year and that many more to tear them down and store the portable ice rinks! Not only that, the rink is maybe 1/5 the size of the park that used to be flooded, so fewer people can use it. Here is the kicker: it takes 2-3 people with snow blowers each morning to show up and clear out the snow for about 1 hour when it used to be done with one single machine each day. Then, are you waiting? A couple of years later, they only put up 1 of the two purchased portable ice rinks and decided the park needed to be leveled because the ground was crooked and not level so as to make the ice level? Really? So, they rented a backhoe and a number of dump trucks, removed all the grass, and leveled the park so the ice rink could be level? Are you freakin kidding me? Have they not heard of using water? That is self-leveling, just kidding, but what is the difference? They have no Common Sense, and they appear to just be stupid and not held accountable for the taxes they keep raising for stupid and ridiculous projects like this. When you ask them why, there is the typical response, "Because we are the government and we can". This goes on and on and doesn't seem to stop and keeps all of our heads spinning. How do people really think this way? Are they born with such an entitled attitude? It really appears that way all the time when it comes to governments and their addiction to TAX money. Enough is NEVER enough until we all decide to say, ENOUGH is ENOUGH!! And vote these morons OUT OF OFFICE!!

Here is another one that the geniuses in the city council did. They painted lines in the street, to be clear, rainbow lines, in an intersection, to recognize that community. Not that there is anything wrong with that, but did they ask any of the residents, or do they just do any freakin thing they like, on their own time, BUT with our money to appease their inner shortfalls, because if they ask the residents, I am pretty confident, that they would rather save money, than waste money it on some lines with the color of the rainbow, and leveling the park instead of using self-leveling water… LOL. Are you kidding me? No, I am not, because common sense doesn't exist nowadays, in any level of government, Municipal, provincial, or federal, because all everyone wants to do is appease every single individual and political group that exists and their causes instead of being reasonable and responsible. Idiots will be idiots. Why do governments think they are given the mandate to WASTE TAX PAYORS MONEY on stupid things? Ask your local politician next time you see them this question. "WHEN WILL YOU NOT RAISE MY TAXES?" There are so many more examples that I can give you like, the time were they cut the parks grass twice a week, and even on days that it rains. How about when they plow the sidewalks with plows that have scrap up the resident's grass, because they are too large for the sidewalks, and then the geniuses have to go and reseed residents grass because they ruined it with these oversized plows. Geniuses with no common sense!

Let me ask you, if you own a house, why do you pay property taxes, and why do those taxes go up each and every single year? Have you ever thought about that? Have you ever looked at that nice, expensive brochure your town or city sends you with the annual tax rate or mill rate to tell you where the money is going? Why do they have to send you a nice expensive brochure with the TAX Bill to explain to you if it was going for the social safety net? Did you ever do the calculation in regards to how much property tax you pay over your lifetime ownership of your house, compared to renting a house, where you can write off your rent and not pay property tax? Well, let me tell you. The following will probably blow your mind, so please sit down and have a drink close by! I warned you! What more services does your community offer for these increased property taxes, other than to pay for their raises and gold plated pensions. There are no more services they can offer but they will never tell you that but they will tell you they need MORE!!

I have owned a home for 30 years. I started owning real estate in 1990, 32 years ago. I had a condo, where I not only paid homeowner dues but also property taxes. I will give you an opinion on that as well, since a condo occupies air in space, not actual physical land. I started with an annual tax bill of about $2200/year in 1990. I lived in that condo for 12 years until about 2002, when I decided the genius I was to buy a house. So, for 12 years, I paid almost $30,000 in property taxes in some space of air in the sky. There were no services offered as we also had to pay for our own garbage and snow removal, so why were we paying taxes? We only owned some air in the sky? Think about that! I also paid about another $48,000 in that time, 12 years of homeowner/condo fees. I will move on to the next house in a minute, but listen to this COMMON-SENSE about condo living. This will inspire you never to own a space in the sky!!

You buy a condo for a couple of reasons, especially back then, which range from not having to cut grass or shovel snow and upkeep your yard, and also because you want a different lifestyle; owning a house is different than a condo. So you buy a high-rise condo in a building, where in my building, there were 21 floors with 15 units per floor or about 315 homes. If we take an average of the property being about 2 acres or about 4-5 houses in the same amount of land, which would pay a little higher in property taxes, let's say $3000 per year for a total of, let's say $15,000 of property taxes for the same land that 315 units in a condo building are built on. The same condo building pays. Are you ready? 315 x $2500 = $787,000 of property tax. Read that again: a building pays 50 times the property tax than the same number of houses would pay that use the same amount of land. You do that calculation in your head when you realize how many condo buildings are being built where you live, and you wonder, WTF does the city do with all of these taxes? Where do all of these condo "AIR IN THE SKY" property taxes go? None of this makes sense, as a condo owner only owns the air and no real land, yet pays collectively 40-50-60 times the property tax that the same piece of land does that has 5-6 houses on it. Then the government says they don't have enough and keeps raising it because they are providing all of these great services, like garbage collection. Well, geniuses, the condo owner, as stated earlier, pays dues for their garbage to be collected, and snow to be removed so stuff it, the government, with that service excuse. They are ripping people off each and every day, especially condo owners. But COMMON-SENSE doesn't work for someone paying for a piece of AIR either, lol, does it? Maybe next time you think about buying a condo, you may think twice and try to figure out what you are really buying and paying for?

I will continue with the property tax collectively that I have paid to date. So I told you, I paid about $30,000 in the condo "PROPERTY" taxes for the air I lived in, then bought a house, which I have lived in for the past 20 years. In those 20 years, with an average annual tax rate of about $4200, this adds another $84,000 of property taxes. If you add this together, I have paid a net of about $114,000 in property taxes. Think about that for a minute. Think about your situation and compare it to mine. If I put that money each and every year in an investment with an annual return of 5%, I would have, get this, $286,000 of money in my pocket and bank account. Next time a politician knocks on your door, why don't you ask them about property tax, why it exists, and when they will start lowering it? Because of all of those more services they keep giving you each and every year, don't really exist, they are all a lie, because all the services have already been paid for! Good luck, because you are better off banging your head against the wall until the wall gives in because that's when it will stop. The biggest scam and greatest NON-COMMON sense idea that you will experience in your lifetime, but hey, remember, it's for the greater good, all the idiots that can't balance their own checkbooks because it's not their freakin money. IDIOTS, or are we the idiots without common sense and letting them get away with it? They keep asking for more, and there isn't anything we can do about it, because if you complain or ask for an explanation, they will tell you if you don't like it, just move!

A new election is announced, and your local candidates start advertising and putting signs up in your neighborhood. One day, someone knocks on your door, then the doorbell, and after you look at your door camera, you're wondering who this is. You finally decide to open the door, and here we go. This is how most of these conversations go, and/or maybe they should go next time they knock on your door to ask:

"Hi, my name is Joh/Joan Doe, and I am running to represent you in your local area. I have decided to…." Blah, blah, blah, and it keeps going for a couple of minutes. You are curious and let them ramble on for a few minutes until they say: "So, can I count on your vote?" Do they go to school to practice that line so they don't forget and become experts in it? Pardon: "So, can I count on your vote?" You look at them, and by the way, you were just paying your bills just before they showed up, and guess what happened then? Well, you say, how much time do you have for me to ask some questions? They say, "Sure, ask away." I have been living here for almost 15 years, and you know what really bothers me and sticks with me is the amount of property tax I pay and the increase that happens EACH and EVERY year!! Wow, does this person start turning red? "So, let me ask, why do property tax keep going up, and services never change or are reduced, such as the limits on garbage bag collection?" They look at you like deer in headlights. They have no idea how to answer the most asked question that is asked in campaigning. So they will never answer, and they move on and try to pivot to another topic. I think pivoting is also a practiced skill in politics. But some may try to lie to you and pretend they will change it, but you know they are full of crap! But they do say before they leave, "So, with a pause, can I count on your vote?" You look back at them and close the door without answering their question because they couldn't even start answering your questions. You know why they couldn't answer that question is because if they start, they will go so deep down a rabbit hole that they wouldn't be able to get out. They would upset all local unions and other government employees. Because the answer to that question is, "We really don't know why you pay so much in property taxes, and we really don't know why we really need to raise them EACH AND EVERY year, BUT we do because we can, and we have been doing it since the start of time and we need to keep paying for our pet projects, give our employees nice raises, benefits, and gold plated pension, that's why?" That is the real answer, but no one with an ounce of COMMON-SENSE would ever give you that answer because if the unions ever hear them say that, they will be blacklisted so fast, your head would start smoking, and they will lose that union and employee support so fast, like I said, that you may want to think twice!!

The nerve of these idiots. But who are the real idiots? I think we, the taxpayers, are the real idiots who don't hold these elected officials accountable for what they say and what they actually do. Why is it that a politician, it seems, is the only person or people who can lie to your face and not be held accountable? Do that at your job and not meet your numbers or what your job description is, or tell an outright fib/lie and see what happens to you? I am pretty confident you won't be at that job any longer. Taxes, and more taxes, why and when does it stop?

Again, I don't want to keep bashing this topic, but if any responsible government really does work for the people, then they would review each and every decision that needs funding and ask themselves this question: "Would I spend my money on this idea?" or "Is this money a good investment for all our taxpayers?" No politician would spend any money if they asked these questions, but they don't view the taxes they collect as their own money because they have wasted so much of it; what does it matter if it's a few more millions or billions of dollars? We can just put it on the credit card for the future to pay for.

The best is when one level of government feels neglected by another level. Here goes when the City of Toronto has a hole in the budget of almost a billion dollars due to their incompetence and the fact they waste so much money on inefficiencies, such as hiring way too much stuff, plugging potholes each and every year instead of paving entire roads and trying to be everything to everyone, and then at the end of the year, crying to their parents that they don't have any money to pay their credit cards, which they can't carry a balance on, like ten years old. When will these irresponsible people learn that you, as we, the taxpayers, need to live within your needs, and you can be everything to everyone? SO SORRY!!

I don't think there is enough room or time to keep talking about taxes, why they were created, and why they keep being increased each and every year. It might be time for all of us to demand accountability from these governments, and hold them accountable to balance all their budgets each and every year, or call an election and make sure they are not allowed to run for re-election if they don't keep their words.

I want to leave you with this last piece of opinionated advice on this topic of taxes. If you do happen to make real money in this lifetime, do yourself a favor and hire smart people to make sure that you take advantage of all the tax breaks or loopholes that are available to you and your family or business because all of these government geniuses take advantage of them, so why shouldn't you. Because it doesn't matter how much you make, but how much you keep, as the saying goes. We all try to make things easier for the next generation, but not these crazy people. I can go on until I am blue in the face, but this topic really hits home, and the more I write about all the stupidity, incompetence, and non-accountability of these politicians, the more I lose my mind!!

Good luck, and never fight the tax man. LOL..

5: DAILY ACTIVITIES

So, with life, we try to make the most of it. Wasn't it nice when you had no responsibilities and lived with your parents, who paid for everything? You got a part-time job just for fun, and you thought you had all the time and money in the world to enjoy all that newfound money from that part-time job. Then all of a sudden, life creeps up on you, and surprise, you are an adult and had to find your own way in life, rent or buy a home, get a REAL full-time job, pay your bills, and try to figure it all out on your own now, without the daily help of the people that brought you into this world.

There is a lot of life that can be lived, but have you ever wondered why there are so many different things to do, why things cost so much, and what you should pick and choose to spend your disposable income? I use this word loosely: income on, if the government doesn't take it all, first. Make sure you spend it on things you want to do or love to do, as opposed to squandering it on NON-SENSE.

Common Sense! Why pay $250-500 for a hockey ticket and $100 for a baseball ticket to watch a sporting event so you can contribute to a million-dollar employee? Baseball players get paid an average of $7 million hockey, an average of $3.5 million. Not to mention basketball players getting paid an average of $12 million a year. If this isn't crazy, I don't know what is. So what is the difference when you pay $20 for a cinema ticket when the movie costs upwards of 100's of millions to produce? Have you ever thought, why are we paying for sports 10x more than we do for the cinema market? Does anyone think this is fair, and do these corporations really care? They keep gouging all of us, and now you can't take your kid to a hockey, baseball, or basketball game without spending a fortune upwards of several hundred dollars. That's if you can even find a ticket to the event, because most are sold out to big corporations and ticket scalpers!

We all like to either go to a movie or maybe a sports event at times, but nowadays, it is way too expensive, as I mentioned. Let's look at the movie business, which I believe most of us love to watch so we can escape some of life's everyday issues and fantasize at times. A movie ticket costs $20, plus, who can go to the movies without buying popcorn, a soda, and maybe a sweet? Now we are at $30-35 for those items, and now we are at about $50-60 for a movie, and that's only for one single person. Say you take your spouse and 2 kids. Now we are talking almost $150-175 bucks for a movie. You remember above when I said you were living with your parents because life caught up, and a movie was $5, and popcorn and soda were $7.50. Why so much increase in these prices when most theaters don't even have people selling tickets anymore, and now you have to self-serve through an app? How and why do these places get away with it? But we still keep going; maybe not as often as before, but we still do. Lets face it, we need to enjoy some things in life that are simple and let us dream, don't we?

Let's move on to a sporting event that you may want to attend because it's only once or twice a year. Let's pick a hockey game. A cheap ticket will cost around $75, with all the additional costs like the following. Parking is $25. A beer is $15, some peanuts or popcorn is $20, and a hotdog is $10. If you add this up, we are talking $150 for a single event ticket. If you want to, let's say, enjoy yourself. If you take one kid only, we now are talking $250 bucks. Are they crazy!? Or are we crazy, and now, who has any common sense? It certainly isn't us, the people, that will pay this kind of price to watch a sporting event for 2-3 hours!! Wow!! Crazy!! But some of us do it and will continue to support these greedy corporations!

Forget about going to a sporting event. How about trying to put your kid, if you are lucky enough to have one or two, in a sport, let's say hockey. I am sure you know where I am going with this. From skates, $100, to pads, $100, to a couple of sticks, $200, and to the registration fees, who the hell really knows where they go except to circumvent Hockey Canada and all their scandals? This really adds up. This isn't mentioned if you have an older kid who needs to travel to hockey tournaments and other games, where you may need to drive for hours and also obtain hotel rooms and other expenses. This really adds up, and you wonder why life is hard because who doesn't want to do all they can for their kids, especially if they want to join these sports or clubs? Where does all this money go, and whatever happened to flooding the skating rink in the park, more on that later in the government section above as I mentioned, and allowing your kids to play for "FREE" and if they were really interested, then maybe we can get them involved in these activities. Everyone thinks we are made of money, and no one uses COMMON sense, except if you complain to the government, and they subsidize your usage because you will shout racism if they don't!

Let me move on to trying to take a trip with your friends and or your family. Since when does booking a hotel, where you sleep for a night, and maybe use for a couple of hours, with a shower or so, and now most are $200-300 a night, on the low end. Who in their right mind can afford this? Try booking a hotel for 3-4 nights, and it will cost you $1000 bucks, and that doesn't even include food or drinks. When did these hotel chains think that we all make this type of money? Does anyone use any COMMON sense? Then, these hotel geniuses advertise their rooms on apps that shop their rooms at lower rates because we are all TOO stupid to realize that we can't search these sites and find these lower rates ourselves. Then try to get some food at one of these places. Listen, let me tell you, they are not 5-star hotels, but they think they are. You order a couple of $25 burgers, and they ask you if you want fries or a salad with that, and you think, no, it's not extra, is it, and they say, $5 for fries, or $6 for salad, and you say WTF!!! So, for a couple of nights of getting away with your spouse and kids, you just dropped $1500, and you are not even in a hot weather place. You are only a couple of hours away from home. Do you think this can't be right, and then it all makes sense, or does it!! COMMON SENSE, think not!

The fall comes around, and as any sports fan knows, when the fall hits, it is NFL season, every single Sunday. But don't tell that to your spouse. Sometimes, you wonder if you can take Sundays off from your relationship, being married or not, so you can enjoy the NFL with your buddies, beer, and chicken wings. Your significant other says, "Isn't the Super Bowl enough for you and your friends?" You think, really, we need to get to that game, and there are many, many weeks of games to go. Do we stop you from watching your soap operas, or The Bachelor, for that matter? Come on, significant others (this is the politically correct side of me), can you use some common sense here because we need a break also at times? I love my football, and so do millions of other guys, and we really need our NFL time. That's all I will say about this as it's a sore spot for a lot of my friends, as it seems that something always comes up each and every Sunday, as it did for me this year. Wow, even if I wanted to watch, I couldn't believe how many other people don't have any common sense by scheduling events on NFL Sundays!! Wow, this really gets my goat, if that's even an expression.

It's important, and I believe vital, to live a long and healthy life, to take up some type of physical activity, such as joining a health club, joining a recreational team sport, or whatever you think is important to you, and makes you happy. This type of interaction not only keeps you active, but it keeps your mind active and healthy as well by interacting with other people. As I stated, Humans need other Human interactions to make our lives meaningful.

I have done and currently still participate in a number of different activities that keep me active and healthy, and one of the mainstays is going to the gym on a regular basis. But one of the issues I have that makes no COMMON-SENSE is why a gym membership charges you extra money just for signing up. This really bothers me and others as well when you have to pay an annual membership fee. Why is this? You go and try to join a Gym, and you talk to one of the salespeople, and they start telling you how great their facility is compared to other places, and your head starts to spin when they give you all the payment options, and available EXTRA services, from towel to water? Really? Then they say something like: " It will be a $199 initiation fee to start, an annual membership fee of $99, and a monthly fee of $50.

Hmm, really. Common sense doesn't seem to exist in Health clubs or gyms because I think that they all think we are stupid GYM rats, even in our older age. Why the hell would I pay an annual fee when I pay a monthly membership fee?

I could go on about this and all the other absurd items we deal with daily, but no one seems to have any common sense because they couldn't answer the question: Why an initiation fee and why an annual fee? They look at you like, "Because they all pay for it, that's why"!

I will leave this topic now as it's quite frustrating to me and others as to the fees and charges and other types of payments we seem to be asked for without any real explanations. I will leave this with you, though. Please look into activities and other types of hobbies that keep you moving and active. You will appreciate it in your later years when your health, for most of us, will start to deteriorate, but we can help slow this process both physically and mentally with these hobbies and activities. Take something up, anything and everything ranging from simply daily reading of a book to taking regular walks in the park to appreciate like. Use COMMON-SENSE people, and keep your body and mind in shape. You only have ONE!

Now to WORLD POLITICS and the corruption we all live in and live with because there is no such thing as a democracy, no matter what all of these Politicians tell us!!

6: WORLD POLITICS

So you turn on the Television, and you see all of the issues in the World. As stated previously, Inflation is skyrocketing, gas prices have gone up 50-60%, food prices are going up dramatically, and everything you need, not want, is affecting the money, if any, you have left over each month. You keep looking at your bank book, and it's going down, and you look at your credit card bills, and they keep going up. Why?

You keep wondering what your local government is doing, aside from spending more money on nonsense, to help you. You know what, nothing because they don't really care and forget what their purpose in life is!!! Idiots, all of them.

Why is this happening? Well, let's have a closer look at this. Every government in the world is blaming the Russian War on another corrupt country, Ukraine, but is that true? Inflation started to increase early in 2021, with the slow and steady creep of gas prices due to the new government in the USA, as on DAY 1, the New POTUS, who doesn't seem to know what day it is most of the time, signed an executive order to stop the Keystone pipeline which would affect the oil flow into the USA from one of the world's largest oil producers, Canada, which also affected Canada's economy and GDP.   But did anyone say anything except congratulations, Mr President!! As I stated, there is a deeper reason for all of this peril we are all experiencing now around the entire globe! He also rescinded a number of drilling permits that no one in the USA wants to speak about except those special interest groups. So oil is bad now, even though it touches 60-70% of the products we use in the world, if not more. Does anyone really understand or realize what is occurring around the world, or who is running the world's most powerful nation, the USA? It appears either they know and don't care, or they are all in on this redistribution of power and money that is currently occurring. We better get a hold of what is happening before it's too late to do anything about it! We are all in this together in the western world, all politicians and governments are lying to us!

But no one really made a big deal about it, including the country I live in, because we have a bunch of drama people running this country also. Why would we complain to the USA about affecting the Canadian economy by canceling Keystone, as our economy is dependent on this and is about 60% of our GDP? What was the impact of this on the Canadian economy? Not much because the oil we produced was either trucked or railed to the USA for processing. And the additional oil that couldn't be serviced in that manner was freighted to, guess who, CHINA through ocean freighters, causing, you guessed it, more pollution. But no one will tell you this. So, if Canada didn't slow down the production of oil, why did prices start going up and then affect all aspects of daily living? Let me tell you, using COMMON SENSE, as no other government will, that this doesn't make any sense. If we were exiting the "PANDEMIC" and oil prices were stable, why, before the war, did prices start rising? Well, it was all artificial and was driven by future contracts that no one wanted to talk about or even knew about. This is where all the big money guys play roulette with all of our lives, gambling to raise prices on everything from oil, corn, wheat, currencies, and everything you can think of to make up all the losses they sustained when oil went to $6.00 a barrel. Do you remember this? Well, look it up: $6.55/barrel at the start of the pandemic, unheard of in the past! They all lost their shirts, billions of dollars for several days and weeks. They figured, let's get it back, and oil, with the Keystone announcement, was the right time to manipulate the market back to crazy prices. They stole it all.

All governments are intertwined in one way or another. Some governments will tell their citizens, but most won't because there are a lot of backroom agreements and deals being done without any concept as to how it may affect the everyday person who just wants to live and enjoy their life. World Politics is a game to most of these countries, as is the board game RISK, and most of these world leaders don't give a crap about what they do and how it affects their people, but it continues to happen because no one is held accountable to any decisions, good, but mainly bad, that their government makes with other corrupt governments. Most citizens don't even understand why your government meets with other ones around the world on a regular basis. Why do they meet and what is discussed? No one is ever really told, and only is told when reporters ask the questions that are important to their country. Most politicians, unfortunately, don't answer the questions truthfully but with half truths so it doesn't upset the voters!

They are changing the landscape of society, all Western governments, but specifically the leader, the USA government, so they can implement something they call the NEW GREEN DEAL, that all the left-wing lunatics think will save the planet, but will destroy human civilization, because the geniuses don't remember the majority of the population needs oil and gas to heat their homes in the winter or they will freeze to death, just like the ice age. COMMON SENSE, morons!! They want to propel us into poverty while they lift the most dangerous society, China, by buying all of these solar panels and electric batteries from them, which will, in NO WAY, heat our homes or charge the batteries they sell us. They are going down a road that will bankrupt western civilization, but they don't care because they all have set themselves up with all the corruption they are involved in. Hence all of these summits, ranging from G7 TO G20. Do they really accomplish anything for the greater good? Not really?

As I stated earlier, all world politics are intertwined, and that being said, why is Canada so dependent on the USA for gas when Canada is the world's #5 oil producer? Did you know that Canada doesn't have very many gas refineries in Canada, to service our consumption and oil production? And if we do, why are our gas prices dependent on the futures markets? They are because it is all a shell game. The people with money drive up prices artificially and make everyone pay more, a lot more, than we have to. No one in power will investigate this because if they did, they would probably find that something smells. Why do gas prices in Canada fluctuate daily, yes daily, not weekly or monthly, like other products? A gas station has up to 7 days' worth of gas in its holding tanks, yet gas moves 1, 2, and 5 cents daily. WHY? WHY? WHY? Everyone with Common sense asks WHY, but people who are in power act stupid, put their heads in the sand, and do nothing, stating it's the market conditions. Supply and demand is the phrase they always use, thinking we are all uneducated people. If gas stations and oil companies in Canada are not considered to be involved in collusion, I don't know what can be considered collusion. You have one market maker and seller of gas in certain regions that control all of Ontario, where gas prices are exactly the same for over 200 km of radiuses and move the same way each and every day. The only gas stations that make any changes are usually the independents who think they can make a quick buck, but it's all collusion. And no one in Government will investigate this, and you wonder why? If you ask, you are told to shut up, pay your taxes, and be a good Canadian sheep. The Canadian government doesn't investigate because gas generates a lot of taxes for all levels of government, so why cook the golden goose? Gas taxes are one of the most luxurious scams that all western governments invented years ago, so its hidden in the prices you pay each and every time you fill your tank!

Let's move to interest rates. Canada and its political elites keep telling us that housing prices are way too high and inflation is rising, so we need to raise interest rates to fight inflation and try to have a housing correction. Little do they know that there is a limited housing supply in Canada, and raising interest rates only makes BIG BANKS more money and takes more money from our pockets through interest rate increases, which basically siphons money through this interest rate scam, that will do nothing to fight inflation. If a person wants to and can afford to buy a house, the interest rates, now or when they were 20% in the 1980s,s will not deter that person or family. If a home is needed and money has been saved, it will be purchased. The big banks don't produce anything and do not contribute to the GDP, but what they do is steal a lot of our money for the average person through their monthly fees like a ponzi scheme. There is no difference here between Canada's BIG BANKS and the mob. At least with the MOB, you may be able to get a better rate. LOL. Banks take our money and loan it out at high rates while they pay us little interest, if anything at all, and then charge us a monthly fee for keeping it in the bank! Hmm. Who is stupid now and doesn't have any COMMON-

SENSE? It's me and you, fools. Do yourself a favor, if you can, don't play the Ponzi scheme with the Banks, keep your money in your mattress, no kidding, keep only what you need with it, and put the rest in some kind of vehicle that you can earn a return on, such as a GIC, or even better buy an investment property. Borrow from them even more than they want to give you!!

One of the biggest factors that this generation doesn't understand is that history will not work this time. What this means is if you raise interest rates, because you did in the past, to squash inflation, it used to work. But, with people's mindset now, such as living for the present and not for the future, it appears no one really cares. Everyone will keep buying and consuming, and when or if they can't pay their credit cards, they will walk away. With the help of the government and the stress of the COVID pandemic, they will just declare bankruptcy and will not lose their house or cars but will pay pennies on the dollar as reparations to these criminal credit card companies and the Mob, or should I say the BIG BANKS! No one has given this much thought. Rates have almost tripled, and nothing, gas prices, food prices, and all other consumables, have skyrocketed and keep going up. No one will stop lying to us. They are doing something that is hurting us all because what is inflation really, and who is it really hurting? Does anyone ask the question as to why inflation needs to be at a 2-3% rate? Where did all these smart people pull that number from? Why do they feel 2-3% inflation is acceptable or needed at a time when governments are making us in Canada pay more through their nonsensical scams, like the CARBON TAX, which is just a tax grab that accomplished ABSOLUTELY NOTHING? All of what the world governments are doing is a money and wealth shift so they can control their citizens and make us feel that we need them. Governments are the creation of the people, and sooner or later, this will come to fruition, just like it has through thousands of years of history, by either revolutions or assassinations! Look in history how things really change, and those are the only 2 ways they really change! History has proven this, and the current world wars that are being fought in many countries also proves, change on can happen when push comes to shove and then to war!

Now, with inflation that was created by governments printing and spending money they don't actually have, then, here we go, here comes the war. Now, all these idiot politicians from every single party in the world are blaming Russia for oil and gas prices and inflation. Russia, being one of the world's largest producers of oil, did drive prices up a bit, but most of the increase was due to speculation. If all the countries maintained, if not increased, their production, who cares what happens with Russia? It's all the things all of these swamp people do to pull the wool over all of our eyes. They distract, make excuses, and have word salad press conferences to confuse us even more, to make it look like everything is someone else's doing, aside from theirs. This New World Order of politics and politicians are in this for one purpose only, and that's to make themselves money, A LOT of money. Do you think that continually funding a war that doesn't affect the Western hemisphere at all makes any difference? Well, it doesn't. It's just another excuse for them to throw good money after bad money under the premise it's for the greater good. Have you ever thought, Where are all of these BILLIONS of Dollars actually going? Why does this corrupt country need physical money instead of weapons? Hmm, do you think it ever goes in the front door and out the back door just as fast to some of these politicians'

Swiss bank accounts? Think about it!! Use your common sense, folks!! None of it makes any sense. You have one of the world's greatest powers, Russia, trying and can't take over a little nation that means nothing and has no defense department or army? Why is this being prolonged, as it has been for almost 18 months, and continues? Can anyone tell you that and or why hasn't there been a negotiated settlement? The answer is that it doesn't benefit the Western world governments or politicians.

I am not sure why first-world countries treat their citizens like this, take advantage of them, and treat them like second-class people by lying and deflecting the fact they have no skills to do the right thing for their people.

So, let's talk some more about a war that affects no one except the 2 countries involved. Why is it so important to all of these politicians? Have you ever asked that question, especially when they keep sending money to one of the world's most corrupt countries? Why is this war, and not the other wars and atrocities, happening around the world, Syria, Africa, and all the other countries fighting for decades, not just for a couple of months? Why is every country sending millions and billions of dollars to Ukraine? Who gives a shit about Ukraine when we can't afford to fill up our cars or buy groceries for our children here in North America? Why is this so important to them? Are they covering something else? Billions and billions of dollars are being sent to Ukraine. Has anyone ever asked, Where is the money in Ukraine? Who is one of the world's largest exporters of grain/wheat and fertilizers? Where is their money, and what have they done since Russia took over Crimea? What have they done? They elected a comedian/actor as their prime minister, yet they have no money or weapons to defend their DEMOCRACY?

Most of the world doesn't care but has to be involved because they are all reliant in one way or another on the USA for handouts. The USA hands out so much money to many governments around the world that people aren't aware of so they can receive favors back when needed. There are so many other issues to deal with or should I say worry about in other countries, such as Iran and their bomb-making, North Korea and their missile launching, and China and their manipulation of the world supply chain, but all they want to talk about and the fund is the Ukraine and Russian war. Why? There are a lot of other things that can be and need to be addressed by all the world's governments and politicians, but they don't, and you have to wonder why. Or are you too busy trying to survive while the Canadian government keeps stealing your money by raising your taxes? There are a lot of issues in the world that affect your daily life, like the supply chain that limits the medicine you can get for your kids, but no one is doing anything about it. We keep relying on third-world countries for products we buy and consume daily instead of bringing back this manufacturing and supply chain to North America to benefit our country and citizens. This should be the first topic of discussion with Western political leaders in both the USA and Canada. Open up manufacturing and invest in our future here! But god forbid if that affects your climate change concerns as it's not close to home. Out of sight, Out of mind! Idiots, all of them without common sense. Manufacturing is the life line of civilization, but its being ignored in North America. We need to bring back this important industry instead of relying on China, Thailand and Turkey to make things we, in North America need and want. But crickets from all our leader and politicians. Have you ever asked why? Is all we need in Canada are coffee shops and burger joints to service our economy? Hmm, no Common-sense here!!

Each country in this world has its own issues to deal with. Each country seems to have very corrupt, so-called elected officials stating they are looking out for the best interest of their citizens. If this is the case, why are there so many issues and descents in each country? Each country and each citizen is struggling to put simple food on the table when they work 40-50 hours a week, yet every politician is living like the Gatzbys, traveling the world, and expensing everything because the citizens pay for these expenses when most if not all, are non-sense and are NOT needed. Governments collude to make it difficult for their citizens to make life better and easier, and when citizens find a way to generate wealth, every government in the world tries to take more of that wealth away from their citizens in the form of raising taxes. Generations try to make life easier for the next generation, but now these idiot politicians, who can't live within their means, are looking to implement an inherence tax as if the amount they steal from us isn't enough. Every government is out to oppress its citizens and make them all dependent on government handouts, so we all have to rely on these morons. From pensions to health care, they are controlling it all and telling us we need to contribute more by scaring us and wasting millions and billions of dollars on boondoggles that no one is held accountable for. When COMMON SENSE prevails, boom, the government will make up some excuse, like we need to pay reparations to some minority group for things that were done to them by our great, great grandfathers, and that's only if you were born in Canada, but no one seems to again, ask the hard questions as to WHY, all of these regressions need to be dealt with. Why can't they be left alone and live and enjoy the life that was promised to us by GOD and not the government? They want to waste our money on this idiotic nonsense and make themselves feel good. Why the "F"don't they put all of these questions on a referendum and ask the citizens what they think? Reason? Because the truth hurts, and all of these politicians will be put in their place and be voted out. Citizens are smart yet are truly oppressed by scaring us all into thinking governments know better! Really? Don't you think so?

Have you ever wondered why your country, Canada, or the USA, depending on where you live, cares more about other countries than their own people who pay their taxes, so they can be squandered on non-sensical ideas and projects? Our PM gives away money like it's candy. Here is $25 million because you had a flood or earthquake in your country. Here is another $100 million because you have no security in your country. Does it not upset you or at least baffle you why this is being done without any accountability for all of this money? We never see what happens to it while we are struggling to pay the taxes that are raised every year by every level of government in Canada. They waste it and then come running back to the well and ask for more because they can, as we have no other choice but to pay it at source. Again, why does Canada, and USA fund all of these third world countries? They do because we, the western Hemisphere, oppress these countries as well, by not allowing them to enter the twenty first century with the new technology or tools to succeed on their own!

There are other countries in this world that seem to get along fine with their governments and the fact they stay out of their lives and pockets. You have a lot of countries in Europe,

South America, and even Africa that seem to enjoy their lives, even though they may not have the same wealth, health care system, or social safety nets of North America. But why is this? Do you ever wonder? Well, let me share with you my opinion. A lot of these countries only know what they know, and they are not raped like we are in Canada, where we pay up to 60% of our money in one form or another in taxation and then struggle to survive. These countries may not have the best health care, schools, or other things that we do, but everything comes with a price, and you sometimes have to wonder if the price we pay here is really worth it. That is especially true when we see what all these levels of government do with our money and how they treat us with their condescending arrogance.

Why do all these countries hold all of these summits and get-togethers, as stated earlier, so as to discuss ideas that you wouldn't discuss yourself at the kitchen table because you think that they are idiotic? But then they commit to implementing these ideas, and guess what? Our 1st world country seems to think that it's a good idea they take your money and invest it in these ideas without an ROI or any commitment to improving our lives. It appears that we are blessed and should appreciate what we have, even though most of us work hard each and every day for what we have. But it appears some, if not most, government officials think they have an unlimited credit card that they can use at their discretion without any accountability. Politics and politicians around the world must all attend the same training and schools that teach them all how to screw their own citizens. That must be it, because that's all that makes sense, and that's all they have in common. They are all magicians, and they seem to keep pulling the wool over all our eyes regularly.

So don't be fooled when you hear we live in the best county with the best health care and living conditions in the world because all of these affect not only your financial health but your physical and emotional health as well. Take a trip abroad and judge for yourself if you have the finances to do so; you will be shocked both in a good way and bad way, and then judge for yourself if our politics and governments work for you!!

You may be surprised by other living conditions and mindsets in the world. Common sense exists, but it may not be in the country you live in. Next time a politician talks to you, just remember that most, if not all of them, are always lying to you because they can !!! Idiots!! Remember, every time their mouth opens, there is a new potential lie that they are emitting!! LOL

7: WOKENESS AND IT'S STUPIDITY??

Who freakin cares, Or do we still call it cancel culture??

Where or how do we start with this topic? First, we had Me Too. Then I believe we morphed into Cancel culture, moving into Wokeness, and maybe Reparations, DEI, CRT, and we can keep going because society has lost its way and thinks making all of these new ideologies or talking points can change the vast majority of the North American Society. Let's face it: third-world countries and others don't really care for our stupidity. We are causing our own destruction with all of this non-sense and trying to appease everyone which is impossible.

Let's see. COMMON SENSE. Really people, why don't smart, or should I say seemingly smart people, want to admit that there are only two, yes people, 2, 2, 2, genders. If you forgot, there are males and females. That's all the higher power or whomever you believe in created. That's it. Sorry, people, for offending you, but there are not more than 2 genders in the human race. You can cut or slice things off and pretend to be something or someone else, but again, only two exist. If there are more, please, please educate me because in my more than 5 decades of existence, that's all there has been, and that's all there will ever be. That is, unless, a higher power, maybe from outerspace shows up with another gender, or species? This may change if we are invaded by aliens, possibly, or maybe we already have been invaded by a bunch of alien lunatics, and that is why they are all acting like morons without a brain. Why do so many people, that are so educated not want to admit this?

How ignorant or stupid can a Supreme Court judge want to be in the USA or politicians in Canada, pretend to be, when they can not answer the question, "What is a woman?" Please define a woman. Her answer, "I'm not a biologist?" Are you freaking kidding me? A Supreme Court judge in the most powerful country in the world acted like an ignoramus because she didn't want to offend someone or a group of people she thought may have offended, but she should not be in a place of power with such a warped view of simple topics. Should you be a person who makes life-or-death decisions when you can't be honest and true to yourself or the people you were appointed to protect by not defining what a woman is? Many people in power, seem to lose their minds and in this case, their COMMON-SENSE, when they are asked a very simple question. They appear to want to overthink or pretend they are smarter than the average person. Why? This is where we are in this world. We are allowing these idiots to determine what and how we think because they are driving some sort of power-grab agenda that will just divide and segregate society even more than it already is due to the power-grab of North American politicians. All of these people should be voted out of office, and in some cases out of society. Why do they refuse to keep dividing the public? What is the underlying agenda in ALL of these cases as it appears to be the same. People without Common-sense are running North American politics and stealing our history and money and destroying this world!

It appears, according to some people, there are more than 2 genders, and for you people that may not like this, they keep inventing all of these stupid pronouns: he, she, they, them, me, I; and whatever else you idiots want to pretend you want to be! Stop kissing everyone's ass and realize what you are doing to contribute to this society that is disintegrating and losing all of its principles and fabric. People fought and died for our freedoms, and here we are, pretending that there are more than 2 genders. How many people died protecting our freedoms, and now we are insulting all of them by living in a fantasy world? If you really are true to yourself and the greater good of society, all of this nonsense would stop, and we would try to make people's lives easier and less controversial. Yes, lets accept everyone for who they are, but lets again stop pretending that men can have babies? Idiots all of them!

There is a case in Canada amongst other place as well, where a student in a Catholic school system has been suspended because they refuse to acknowledge more than 2 genders. How can this be possible in the time we live in? Did Adam and Eve create more than 2 genders? That is, if that is even true, according to some. Don't get me wrong, if you want to identify and make something up, by all means, knock your socks off, but don't think for a second you can sell your crap to the rest of us. The mainstream will let you do and say whatever you want and identify as you want, but that doesn't mean you can change how the majority of the world quantifies this in history because, sorry to tell you all, there are only 2 genders, like it or not, male or female, and if you want to identify as another, as I stated go ahead. If you want to identify as another, no one is stopping you, but respect others positions as well, because the majority does have common-sense, unlike the minority who pretends to live in this Utopic world!!

Now, we get into the subject of these idiots who say men can have babies. There are leaders in the world's most powerful country, the USA, and some of these morons, not to insult real morons, tell you that men can give birth in the human gender. Never, and I mean never, has this ever happened. If you ask 100 scientists and doctors if this is possible, 101 will tell you you are an idiot. And yes, 101, I meant that to make a point, as there is no one on this earth who is normal and has half a brain and can actually look at you in your face or in the mirror and tell you this is possible. Yet we have public-voted leaders in power, tell you this. And these morons are also teaching our children this nonsense. YES, I said it, NON-SENSE. This is done because people are really getting tired of being normal or striving for a better life, and in my opinion, have given up. And instead of just giving up, they make this crap up and stir the pot for their own financial gain. COMMON-SENSE people, because this will come and bite you in the ass sooner or later, or maybe some of you may like that.LOL. I believe there is one species in this world where the male does give birth, and that is the Seahorse and Sea Dragon. Go figure, these individuals might want to identify as one of those species on this earth, and then yes, maybe a male can give birth. But people, why don't you grow a set and stand up for what is right and what is really silly or stupid!! Again, be accepting of everyone, because its always better to be a good person as opposed to a bad one, but also keep in mind what reality really is, and its not about more than 2 genders! Period!

We have people promoting dividing classes based on, get this, sexual preference. Whatever happened to the segregation movement of the 20s and 30s, now we think we have moved on and provided everyone with the same opportunities and respect, except to get to this point of sexual segregation. They want straight people to graduate with straight people and others to graduate with others, yet they seem to forget we all live in the same world. They think by doing this, they would gain more power and acceptance, which is total nonsense. People have been accepting of others for generations. I am not saying all people are accepting, but the majority of us are because we are caring, and we believe in the human race and being compassionate to our fellow humans, regardless of what or who you choose to be. But they still have to make themselves feel that they are superior by doing these silly things. We all deal with issues in life and struggle with internal demons; all of us do, but we find a way to move forward and be good people. Why are these, mainly politicians, promoting this type of division as a divide-and-conquer attitude? They should look at history because when this has occurred in the past, it usually bites them all in the ass, and they eventually fall and burn or are burned. Common sense and history don't seem to have taught these idiots anything. All western politicians should have to study history, and the rise and fall of all of the previous superpowers, before they are allowed to enter into any political race, maybe that will teach them some common-sense!

We make accommodations for these people in all aspects of life, from trying to provide different working arrangements to bathroom facilities to health benefits. We raise flags to acknowledge them, pay for their parades and that seems to never be enough. Now they demand, being one gender, to use the other gender facilities. Why!!! Dammit!!! Why!! We provide family and other designated areas, but they kick and scream discrimination because, in my opinion, they can't handle their situation and need everyone in their world to acknowledge them. Hence, let's go to the human rights tribunal and cry until we get our way. We cry, and then they give in because we cried as kids, and our parents gave in, and we figure, let's do it as messed up adults and see if they still give in. Not taking into consideration the other 99.9% of people that crying will affect. They don't give a rat's ass about other people, which is the majority of society, yet they pretend to because by getting their way, they make everyone else in that room uncomfortable. But, hey, who cares!!! Then they say they have been discriminated against at other events, like comedy clubs, sports events, or characters in movies, and then run to court to sue people because they know, by the precedent that has been set, they will win, and usually it's not about principle, but about money. They don't care if they ruin someone else's life, business, or anything else as long as they get their own way. Kick and scream, like two-year-olds, because their feelings were hurt, because someone said something to them they disagreed with, and let's see if we can make their lives better by screwing others. There should be human rights for normal people, maybe it should be called the COMMON-SENSE TRIBUNAL FOR HUMAN RIGHTS!!

These people keep trying to convert people to their thoughts and way of life, and again, they don't care how or who they hurt or offend. They want to be accepted and keep asking for rights that have been given to them, such as marriage and benefits, but they keep insisting they are not being recognized and keep asking for the limelight. To be dealt with in their own world, and maybe we can all bow and salute them.   And low and behold, we give in to them throughout the whole world by allowing parades and other functions even though they represent the vast minority. Yes, sorry to tell you all, these people who want to identify as other genders are the MINORITY. Maybe less than 1% of 1% of the world's population of 8 BILLION people. Yet, when straight, or should I say heterosexual people, or people with COMMON-SENSE, want to throw a parade or something, they cry and kick and scream because it doesn't cater to their needs, and god forbid they don't agree with being not like them. Why is it? I can't celebrate my sexuality, yet my hard-earned tax dollars are used, wasted, and spent on these other people, the minority, so they can raise a flag and keep telling us all that we still don't accept them, even though, they have been doing it for decades, if not almost half a century. Why don't we stop celebrating a minority group and start celebrating the HUMAN RACE? Do you know why? Because idiots run this world, and none of them have any COMMON SENSE or any balls to not be so politically correct. And they feel empowered to spend your hard-earned tax money on this stupidity, and then they say they are running a deficit and tell you that you need to pay more taxes because they ran out of money. You ask why, and they say. 'I don't really know, but you don't have a right to ask, just pay more" idiots. COMMON SENSE, WHERE IS IT!!!!

Now, let's get to a topic near and dear to my heart. Sports, or should I say, woke sports. When is a woman, not a woman, when she can compete with the men?? Sorry, that doesn't and really can't happen, can it? We all know it can't because estrogen can't compete with testosterone. We all know that. Maybe I shouldn't assume we all know that because there are exceptions to the rule. But testosterone can definitely compete and beat estrogen. Please don't take this the wrong way, ladies, but it's true that 99% of the time, at the highest levels, a man will always be faster and stronger than a woman because that is the way we are composed physically. So, a woman isn't a woman when they were born a man with testosterone. Who the crap are these people trying to kid? A man competing against women? Is that right? Of course, it's not, but why do all of these idiots think it's ok? So we don't hurt the little snowflakes and their feelings. This whole thing with these male swimmers and track and field sprinters competing against and winning every single event against women and girls is completely and totally wrong. Who the crap thinks it isn't? Everyone that has NO COMMON SENSE? Are they all idiots? Hell yea. How can a woman compete against a man in a physical activity or sport at the highest level and have any chance to win? It's just not possible. We are made differently. Are there special women out there that are gifted? Probably, and of course, there are, but in almost all cases, 99.9% of professional male athletes will always beat a female professional athlete. But a professional male athlete should beat a professional female athlete 100% of the time. Now, we have males who are mediocre, at best, crying in their breakfast cereal and competing against women. Guess what, geniuses, they will win 99% of the time. But they all shut their eyes and say, hey, it's fair because they are taking, get this, testosterone, reducing medication. WTF. What are you talking about? You can't eliminate testosterone in males; try all you want. You bunch of lunatics!!! What makes women different than men? I am totally embarrassed to be a male when females are losing everything from scholarships and medals and money to males who would never, ever win against another male but will always win against a female. Shame on you all who propagate and tolerate this craziness.

The issue with the above situation is it's affecting so many girls who have dreams and aspirations to excel in sports, and they are now being infected by non-female girls, from swimming to athletics. This is not right. A girl should be able to compete against biological girls, and it should be fair and not be poisoned by this nonsense. For all you crazies out there who probably don't have the guts to speak up because you may offend the odd snowflake out there, why don't you do the right thing and speak up and stop putting your head in the sand and pretend it's not happening? Biological Men should compete against Biological men, and biological women should compete against biological women. And there should be no discussion about it because anyone with half a brain would understand the majority, not all, but 99% of men will always outperform women in athletics of any kind that involves speed or strength. It only makes sense. But hey, we are going down a rabbit hole that will be difficult to get out of if this continues to happen. Let's try to stop it, and all of you enablers should be ashamed of yourselves. Every one of you who thinks this is right definitely doesn't have children, but you are pushing an agenda that will come back to haunt us all, and you won't like it either when it comes back to affect you because, eventually, it will, YOU BUNCH of FOOLS and IDIOTS. Common sense, you were born with it, so use it, especially in this case!! Let a boy be a boy and a girl be a girl until THEY may change their minds. But please don't interfere with something you have no knowledge of. You should all be ashamed of yourselves for letting this happen. No one is stopping boys and girls from playing together. Most of us, if not all of us, did this while we were growing up and really didn't give it much thought.

This should still be happening, but not at the elite level, as we are all looking to enjoy the simplicity of life. Let the professional and very competitive athletes compete against their own born genders. It's as simple as that, people. Why is this being accepted in the North America circus is a question that all politicians need to answer? Why are we not using Common-sense, and let nature dictate what we have known in this field for generations? Please everyone, do the right thing and not let this continue, as its WRONG!!

I am going to move on to some other examples of cancel culture that are affecting aspects of life that may surprise you. I am going to let you know what happened to one of my friend's kids, and you tell me if this sounds right. Common Sense or sheer stupidity and ignorance. My friend's son is in grade 5, and they were all told that they will not be able to wear Halloween costumes this year due to more ethnic kids being in the school who don't recognize Halloween. He asked the teacher why. He was told that a decision was made and that he needed to accept it and not make a fuss. When he asked for a better explanation, he didn't accept it and said, don't we live in a democracy, and should we vote on it? So, he asked his classmates to raise their hands if they wanted to wear a costume this year, and every single one of them raised their hands. Then, the teacher called the principal, and the boy was suspended from class for a week. He went home, and his mom asked what happened. He explained it, and she couldn't believe it, so she called the school to find out if the story was true, no costumes this year? She was told a number of parents complained to the school, so she asked how many, and the principal slipped and said, 2? WTF? So, there are no costumes for the kids because we have become so WOKE with cancel culture, and now we do not have any COMMON SENSE to save your life. Now, kids can't be kids, and they can't wear their costumes in school because some complain! Wow. Cancel culture is more prevalent than we know, and each and every day, we are bending over backward in North America to accept other cultures that we forgot that we have rights and historical norms as well that should be respected and not canceled to accommodate the minority and not to offend a few.

The above two examples should scare us all because, again, we are going down such a big rabbit hole that we will never be able to reverse course until it's too late. A lot of people have gone simply crazy, and I think the reason why is that they really did lead a bad childhood and don't want to leave any snowflake behind. Why should we accommodate every single person in this world, the very small minority, and I do mean a very small minority, that is affecting every person in every part of our daily life? This is the most NON-SENSICAL and totally stupid thing we are all accepting, but to be honest, it seems there is nothing any of us can do to change or fix it. Be careful because one day, we will all wake up to this 'bizarro world of life. All of this wokeness is out of control, and needs to stop because all it does is add fuel to a fire that is brewing in North America, as most people are fed up with all of this non-sense, and it will blow up one day to the point that we all hate each other because of these IDIOTIC POLITICIANS who have NO common-sense and don't do what they were voted to do!

I am going to share an experience that kinda "freaked" me out. I was out during the holidays at a mall, which shall remain unnamed when I needed to use the facilities. This mall is very large, and it was quite difficult to locate one, but when I did, I walked down this hallway looking for the image instead of the words because everyone thinks pictures are better than words, man or woman, male or female. Really?? I walked past one entrance that had no pictures, kept going to the end, and started walking back when I still didn't see the picture or the words I recognized. I must have had a confused look on my face because someone standing there said, "It's all in one now," while he seemed to be waiting for someone. I said, " What's all in one?" He said, "The washrooms." I said, " Hell, NO!" But since I needed to go, I walked in very hesitantly. I thought, F, this is really freakin weird. Why?? Why?? Why is this being forced down our throats?

I did my business and noticed girls and women putting on makeup and others, and I found this very uncomfortable. I really didn't know what to make of it. I decided to write the mall to voice my opinion that I didn't think this was right, especially since less than 1% of 1% of the population identifies that way, and why are we so accommodating to such a few while really making it very uncomfortable to the majority? It appears this is the number 1 goal of society and all these left-wing nuts. COMMON-SENSE people, the majority, and I mean high majority, want to still have the separation of genders, like it or not. Get it through your thick skulls, you few idiots who make these stupid decisions. I don't want to use a washroom that girls or women, young or old, use also. I don't need to see tampons and other non-male items in a men's washroom. Why do we need to do this? What was wrong with men/women, male/female washrooms? We always had a family facility, and people who don't identify on one side or the other are welcome to use the family one. We are messing up this world to the point of no return and no on can seem to tell us, NORMAL, folks, Why? But the question should be WHY?? Why is this happening to the majority of the world? Some of these people running these organization don't seem to understand until its too late. Can you say, Bud Light, Target and a few others that have lost billions because the CEOs of these companies don't seem to have any COMMON-SENSE to simple life people.

I want to quickly touch on the term "Reparations." I have mixed views about this because, in both Canada and the USA, it appears past transgressions from a long time ago are being addressed by these governments due to the pressure of some small political groups to appease even smaller numbers in our populations. In Canada, we have written checks to the Chinese people who came and built the railroads in the late 1800s because, in the late 1800s, they didn't understand human rights.LOL. Really people. So none of these people are alive, so we paid their descendants this money. This added up to millions and millions of tax dollars because it didn't come out of the politicians pockets but the taxpayer pockets! Because Politicians simply can! We paid the native Indians money because we took their land back in the 1700s and 1800s. We then paid them because they couldn't deal with their children, and the church took them away. Don't get me wrong, that this was totally wrong what happened in this case, but how does money solve anything? We paid other people for being taken into custody in 3rd world countries because they were on terror watch list. We even paid someone who killed someone in a war because he was "mistreated" in Guantanamo Bay prison for murder. There are many more examples, but honestly, when someone is using someone else's credit card, taxpayers cc, they don't care who they give money to and for what reason with no accountability, but then they also apologize " on behalf of the taxpayer" without asking the taxpayer for their input. What a bunch of jackasses and hypocrites. These are the 21st

century politicians who think money, that they don't have, will solve all past transgressions. Little do they know or remember, that all of North America is going BANKRUPT because of these and other Non-sensical decisions these politicians are making, which they were never voted in to make!!

In the USA, they are arguing about giving descendants of slaves money because that affected their future potential in terms of earnings and mental health. I don't agree with slavery, but let's call it for what it is. It was that way in the 1600, 1700 and 1800s, and those people didn't know any better. So now we all have to pay large for transgressions of the ancestors of these countries, even though the majority of Canadians are immigrants and descendants of immigrants. But hey, who cares? Let's give millions and billions of dollars on top of free and subsidized housing and food stamps to people who don't want to better themselves except to hold their hands out and ask for all the freebies they can get. Well, why don't you get a job and see how the majority of society tries to better themselves, instead of complaining and crying " poor me"! Why is the current generation need to do anything but apologize and learn from our history? Why are the so-called political leaders doing this and wasting time, money and energy to keep dividing the North American people, so we feel guilty for our ancetorial transgressions even though it was the way it was done back then, good or bad!! They seem to keep forgetting the bank is bankrupt and by going down these rabbit holes, there will nothing left for our next generation but debt and destruction of our society! Bring down this statues of historical figures, rename schools and do whatever it takes to erase any north American history, but why?

I was going to touch on DEI and other things that some people made their priorities and tried to force down all our throats, but I am not going to. This is because if I do, it's again going to add to that rabbit hole and fuel to this non-sensical fire that is burning, we are never going to escape because once this one is done, there will be the next transgression that someone, the small minority, will make up and want the majority to address. What a joke. Do any of these people have any common-sense and understand what the word "history" really means?

I am not sure if the following belongs in this chapter, but here goes anyway. With all of these negative reactions to all this wokeness, has anyone, specifically the press, ever wondered why they put the word, ANTI, in front of topics they discuss? Here are a couple of examples: anti-black racism and COVID-19 restrictions. Does that sound like a double negative? Or do these people think that putting the word ANTI in front of the phrase that it puts more emphasis on it? Well, you bunch of idiots, it doesn't. It doesn't add more value to the phrase. It really doesn't even make sense. If it's black racism or covid restrictions, that's what it is. There is no ANTI needed, as, in my opinion, it nullifies the whole point you are trying to make. Think of it. Oh, sorry, forgot, you aren't thinking, which is the problem. COMMON-SENSE people, you have it, so please use it.

Why is it that a few select groups of people set the narratives that we discuss on a daily basis, and that pits people against other people? "They" put a 12-year-old as the front person to discuss climate change, and now she is 18, I believe, but no one really realizes how or why that was done. How many 12-year-olds do you think have the platform to discuss a topic like "CLIMATE CHANGE" globally without having some huge group funding her and the agenda? This is discussed in detail in another chapter.

Wokeness is just starting and evolving; if you remember, it started as ME TOO or CANCEL Culture and evolved from there. I am sure long after we are gone, it will include or evolve another bunch of idiot topics or subjects that matter to that generation but really don't impact your daily existence because most people have COMMON SENSE and couldn't give a crap, to put it mildly. All they want to do is live their lives with the Common-sense God gave them!

We have so many poverty and human rights violations in this world from so many countries that we seem to forget what is worth fighting for. Is changing your life and the lives of your family and friends worth it to accommodate a few, or is it worth fighting for child labor rights and other human rights in the rest of the world worth more than allowing Johnny to race against Jane in a track meet, to make Johnny feel that he is superior? Why don't you all freakin give them all ribbons, and we will all be happy and go off to fairyland!! Morons and idiots, all of our political leaders that are manifesting this nonsense.

Our Canadian government feels that we owe it to everyone who complains about anything, the right for them to sue because they have been wronged in some way or another. We have individuals just trying to live their lives with the morals, beliefs, and ethics that they were raised with. If you don't adopt the thoughts and beliefs of others, then you will be possibly charged with a thought crime. Here is an example that just occurred where a Christian was told that they have to acknowledge someone who identifies as neither a male nor female, and because his upbringing taught this sane person that there are only 2 genders in this world, and they would not succumb to this non-sense, because they don't have the right to believe what they were taught, that they were charged with a hate crime and have to spend a lot of money to defend themselves because it seems they don't have a right to their own thoughts or opinions or facts. If this isn't the more insane and NON-COMMON sense thoughts process police, I don't know what is. This is where this Western world is going, and it's going to get even worse. Trust me, because we have the elites running these countries that believe in helping elevate this craziness. What happened to every person who was born with the same rights and can have their own thoughts as long as? I guess everything was thrown out since we entered into this woke non-sense.

We seem to have forgotten what life is about and what should and should not be celebrated and acknowledged. Why don't we celebrate what we believe in, may it be our religion, our lifestyle, or our family, without having people judge us or make an example of us for their benefit? This type of non-sense is eroding our society, as I mentioned, and our history and beliefs, as time will go one and this stuff will get us all in trouble, like stated earlier because one day when we come to our judgment day, you will sit in your chair in your last days of life, and think back, and probably ask yourself, WHY??? WHY?? Next Topic, because this one is very troubling to me and a lot of others.

Now let's move on to another fantastic topic that you may or may not agree with me on. Let's figure it out together and see if the politicians who have made millions and billions of dollars are really pulling the wool over all of our eyes. Chicken Little the sky is falling, or should I say the EARTH IS WARMING!!!

8: CLIMATE CHANGE??

GLOBAL WARMING??

So, do you remember when the ozone layer was shrinking, or a hole was being made in the ozone layer in the 80s, the icebergs were melting, and all the animal species were shrinking and becoming extinct? Well, 30 and 40 years later, all of these pundits made up another crisis. It started with Global warming, where all the crooks made off with millions and millions of dollars, creating a crisis. They released videos, wrote books, and started to spread rumors while at the same time providing limited proof, except that the earth's temperature rose by 1 degree or so. Wow, talk about common sense. Then they all started spending all of this public money, that is, your money, by increasing taxes, and what they started doing, they started to plant trees. Huh!! Wow!! Let's plant some more trees. While at the same time outsourcing all of the world's supply chain overseas so they can increase freight shipping by ocean freighters by over 1000%.

All of these pundits, so-called experts, started warning the world about our extinction a long time ago. In modern history, it started around 1967 by some guy, I believe, named Paul Ehrlich, who warned about our extinction and overpopulation, and then there was "Mr. Spock." Leonard Nimoy, around 1977, did a documentary about us going into the ice age and not being about to inhabit the majority of the earth. Hmm, really, how are these 2 working out today? We move on to the prediction of rising seas in 2000, which will engulf the world by 2020. Then, the beginning of the biggest money grab in around 2005 with the inconvenient truth by the one and only Al Gore, I believe, about the abolishment of civilization and the earth due to global warning, and then climate change, by 2020. Really, Mr Gore? How much money was made with this type of hysteria created by this prediction? I wish we all had a crystal ball so we could all make these types of predictions. LO. Common sense people, please? When the lord decides its time, then its time. Not these loonies! They all made a lot of money. Prediction after prediction, none of these people had been held accountable or asked to return all of the money that they made off of all of these falsehoods.

Ice Free Arctic summers were predicted in 2006 by 2018, if we didn't do something? But what is that something? Hmm, wonder how many of these people lived in the previous ice age? Then there is the world climate guru, John Kerry, who, in my opinion, has never really held a real job but lectures us all about climate change and carbon footprints while he files around the world in his private jets each and every day to every event in the world. Who the hell does he think he is, and what has he ever done besides running unsuccessfully for the White House job? Common People, live your lives and ignore these over-bloated political pundits. He says his job is too important to fly commercial, hence the private jet, which emits more carbon than you will in your lifetime. Here is one of the craziest predictions, where they stated that the Statue of Liberty will be underwater by 2016. All of these people, including Greta, all of them, in my opinion, snake oil salesmen from 1800, causing mass hysteria because they don't have anything better to do with their lives and won't let us live ours without this idiocy. The final nail here is the current president of the USA, who states we are in CODE

RED for humanity, yet he reads a statement like this and doesn't tell you want he or they mean. Really, CODE RED? I thought that was a phrase from the movie A FEW GOOD MEN, with Tom Cruise, and we all know how that turned out. Why do these people continue to do all of this and then not condemn the biggest polluters in this world, China, Russia, and Brazil, but hypocritically keep sourcing all of North America's products and supply chain from these third-world countries who continue to pollute with no solutions?

Everything we have in North America, almost 85% of the supply chain, from clothing to medicine, comes from overseas, using vessels that burn coal and diesel. Hmm, this is interesting, while they all make millions at the same time complaining about Climate change. But they don't tell you that one of the largest polluters in this world are freighters that travel in the ocean. There are over 5000 vessels in the ocean regularly transporting products using these supposedly " dirty fuel sources," adding to climate change. Yet, this never used to be the case when North America was the hub of global manufacturing until all the CEOs became greedy and, with the help of the USA and Canadian governments, moved most of the supply chain to third (3rd) world countries. Yes, the majority of North America's supply chain comes from China and now India. About 85%, to be honest, are from third-world countries. We depend on these countries for medicine for our kids and for all the clothes we put on our bodies. Please say that out loud: Medicine for your kids comes from 3rd world country manufacturers. Why? Because all of the world's CEOs thought that was the only way that they could make their shareholders more money, and wait, that's the way that the CEOs can make all their crazy millions and millions of dollars of bonuses. No one gives a shit about you or me. All they care about is themselves. What other explanation is there for companies to do business with third world countries, who have no human rights for their citizens, except they don't want to pay their own citizens wages that are livable? Why would they want to do business with countries, in most cases, that don't respect human rights? No shit sherlock, why do you think. We do business because none of these assholes have any decency or COMMON SENSE. They forget that we all will die, and what legacy are you leaving, except for people to think you are a bunch of jerks. The common sense gene has been transferred into the greed gene for most of these CEOs and their companies. There is no other explanation for this type of craziness that has obsessed most of the world's largest companies and their GREEDY CEO's.

We all try to do our part, don't we? Buy, recycle, and try to use less, and buy local. But this will not, and does not help anyone because we are all consuming products from overseas, which is contributing to climate change at a far greater speed than any recycling program can handle. Most of the products we buy don't even last like they used when they were built in North America. Everything seems to be throw-aways and last a fraction of the time like they used to. Have you purchased and opened up any box lately with a product, such as a TV, computer, or anything that's susceptible to damage? What is it packaged in? Styrofoam and so much plastic that it takes 2 days to rip it all off. Yet, we can't get a plastic bag now at a grocery store because our Stupid leaders state it contributes to climate change. Are you freakin kidding me? Yet we open thousands, and I mean thousands of these products each and every day in our society, and rip all of this excessive packaging off of all of these products because all the CEOs said that it would be better for their companies to manufacture them in China and other third world countries, as opposed to doing the right thing and making them in North America, like they used to for decades, with less packaging and less pollution and this, just to make more millions for their shareholders and their bonuses. Because, god forbid, these jerks don't make their million-dollar bonuses. Why are we told that we can't manufacture things in north America anymore? Because we can't pay people a decent living wage? Because greedy CEOs want more money? We invented all of these products in North America, and now all these third-world countries are producing them and contributing dramatically to climate change and pollution, and these jerks and hypocrites, get on TV and promote this non-sense. Where is their COMMON-SENSE!! Out the door, I believe, and in their bank accounts!

They talk about reducing emissions, yet the largest polluter in this world is China, and they are not doing anything to curb their polluting. In fact, they are opening a coal plant, according to statistics, every single week! Yes, you heard it here: every single week, the USA is forcing coal plant closures in North America and ignoring the largest polluter in the world, China. Not only are they ignoring them, but they are adding fuel to this fire by continuing to do business with these 3rd world countries. Now, they are moving business to other countries, still third world, such as India, Cambodia, and Thailand, to make more money because China is slowly becoming smarter and starting to increase pricing and costs to their North America allies. All of them crooks and hypocrites, as they don't give one iota of shit, and non of them give a shit or have any COMMON SENSE, that is, if Climate change really is occurring, why do they continue to do business in this part of the world? But don't believe me, look it up yourself, don't listen to the news, take your head out of the sand, and do something about it where you can. Try paying a bit more by trying to buy items made in Canada or at least in North America. Tell all of these CEOs and third-world country hypocrites to go pound salt, if you can, and talk with your money by buying local again. It may not sound like a lot, but it adds up, that's if you can find locally made products. LOL.

All of these idiots will still be getting their brown paper bags full of money envelopes from these third-world countries that don't care about their own people or us by using child labor and not caring about anything except their profits. All they want is to keep their countries and their governments in power by connecting with these highly powerful people.

So "they," as I stated earlier, elect a 12-year-old, I think she is 18 now, to be their token head to complain about the world ending because of climate change. I think they call her "GRETA"? As I stated, how many 12-year-olds do you think sit around with their friends discussing this topic of Global warming, and now CLIMATE CHANGE, REALLY?? She goes on worldwide tours each and every year to promote "their" agenda while she and all others fly on private planes and tell us all, who are just trying to live their lives, that it is all going to come to an end unless we change the way we live. Stop using fossil fuels and adopt power sources that are not reliable in the northern hemisphere to survive. Let's see, stop using gas and oil. Let's see, stop making and eating meat and food that needs fertilizer to be grown. Let's see, stop living in houses and any other building that gives you protection from the elements. What do " they" think we should do? Why don't they stop being hypocrites and let us live our lives and stop polluting the world by doing business with third-world countries that pollute more than all first-world countries combined by transporting all of our goods and consumables over the ocean and back? Is it our fault that man evolved the way we did? Or is it your fault, all of you greedy business people and governments, that outsourced your complete supply chains all the way across the oceans just to make a few more bucks and then pollute the globe by bringing them back using the world's greatest polluting devices, freighters!!! Let's see in the next couple of paragraphs if this makes sense. You can research this and confirm it, as all I am trying to do is educate people who may think this is nonsense.

Have you ever thought about how much carbon is emitted by you driving your car and just trying to provide for your family, compared to these politicians and high profile people that fly around in their private jets weekly, if not daily? Well, let me inform you. A typical passenger vehicle emits about 4.6 metric tons of carbon dioxide per year. Whereas some estimates say, private jets produce 10 times the amount of carbon per passenger. So all these, "so-called " important people" that zoom around to meetings and to entertain you in concerts, and all these politicians going to climate change conferences, for no apparent reason, with hundreds of people, in their entourage, in a lot of cases, are the same ones that say, "Don't drive your gas-guzzling cars, because they pollute, and you should buy electric cars." But they don't tell you that an electric vehicle is not easily available and costs a lot more, about $10-20,000 more than a gas car costs. But that's not the biggest hypocritical statement about buying an electric vehicle. What they refuse to tell you is that most of the charging stations, if they are highly available, that you would use to charge " YOUR ELECTRIC CAR" use fossil fuels to run these charging stations, which they seem to forget. Hypocrites, why don't you use some "COMMON

SENSE"? Renewable energy is not stored energy and can not sustain our existence. Electrical grids have failed horribly when this was tested, as renewables are not dependable sources of energy. When the wind blows, it generates so little energy that it can only sustain a minimal amount for usage. In regards to solar, here is the hypocrisy: the world's largest polluter, yes, CHINA, which is doing absolutely nothing, will manufacture all of the solar panels and then ship them through the ocean for further pollution, but hey, who gives an "F" because all that is important is perception, not reality. Why aren't these solar panels being manufactured in North America if they are so important to our existence? As long as it looks like you are doing something, that's all that matters. WHO, IN THEIR RIGHT MIND, thinks that way, except people that don't think and people that don't have any, you guessed it, COMMON SENSE. They want us to convert to green without having a long-term plan and then give all of our manufacturing to one of the world's most corrupt regimes, China why, because they are all exploiting us and screwing the middle class. But you ask why, and the answer to yourself is, I don't freakin know, and when I ask anyone, they just say, "Because that's what they want." Who the f are they? Did you elect someone that can't explain anything to the citizens of this country because all of them are freakin stupid? Political leadership in North America has been very lacking over the past decade or two, and they are bending over to a communist state because it benefits THEM and not the US!

So, China is going to control the greening of our societies and all of our initiatives? Wow, none of the North American leaders are willing to walk the walk, but they can definitely " Talk the Talk"? Why don't they invest in this manufacturing if they want us to move in that direction instead of pushing our money to a 3rd world country like China? Make the solar panels and renewables here! Are we too stupid to build solar panels in Canada or the USA? Does anyone remember who the world's leading manufacturing countries were?? Anyone? Well, if you don't, here it is: North America developed, designed, and built everything we used in our society until the greedy government bastards sold their souls to China. This was done when China was invited into the WTO in the last 90's and early 2000's. Which also stole our IP and copied everything North American manufacturers designed and built. Why did this happen, and why wasn't it stopped? Because the governments, both the USA and Canada, fell asleep and were tricked into bringing China into the world economy? Now, we rely on a 3rd world country for more than 85% of North America's supply Chain. COMMON SENSE DOESN'T THINK SO. Con job!! I think so!! All of them are crooks and have no brains or plans to bring our backbone, manufacturing, back to North America, where we can be proud to make things and provide good-paying jobs to our citizens. We are the world's smartest and most ingenious countries that built everything until all our leaders lied to us and sold their souls to third-world countries and left our citizens with a service economy and no production at all. But they keep telling us to keep conserving while they live in excess.

Climates may be changing, but the issue here is not this. The issue is no one is telling the world the complete truth. It appears that we all are being lied to in one way or another. We have politicians telling us that we need to stop the use of fossil fuels or we will extinguish our existence, and this will be imminent. Yet, they keep buying goods from 3rd world countries that are the world's largest polluters.

They all want us to either take public transit or buy an electric vehicle. None of them want to tell us the truth about these two topics. Let's discuss public transit, which, let's say, uses electricity. Electricity, in most parts of North America, is fueled by fossil fuels. It doesn't magically appear like some politicians want to believe, and it's not fueled by either windmills or solar panels but by things like coal or diesel. Electric cars are the same. Where do you think that electricity comes from when you need to charge your car each and every day? It comes from a diesel or coal-fired plant in most jurisdictions. Think about this for a second. Let's say you drive a "gas-guzzling car" like a 4-cylinder Toyota. Well, you probably fill that gas tank once a week or so, while someone who drives an electric car really needs to plug it in each and every day, just in case, because you can't always find a non-existent charging station. Each and every day, the vehicle needs to be plugged in while your car is fueled once a week. As I said, in almost all areas of North America, the electrical grids are fueled and supported by fossil fuels because wind and solar can not sustain them consistently and are not reliable sources of energy. But hey, who freakin cares. Buy an electric car, which will cost you, like I said, 10-20K more than a gas car, that's if you can get one. And say thank you to your political leaders who aren't even building charging stations to sustain them!

Electric cars use batteries with lithium and cobalt, just to name a few of the items needed to manufacture these batteries. Here is another topic that no one wants to really talk about. More and more, people are realizing that if your electric car battery needs to be replaced, it appears that this battery costs anywhere from $15,000 to $20,000. Wow. I wonder what it costs to change your gas tank. I really don't know. But that isn't the most important point. It's a fact that no one will tell you what they do with these batteries that go out of circulation and can't be recycled at this time until technology catches up to this need. What really happens to them? Well, we really don't know yet because the electric car is really new to our lives, only coming into existence about 10 or so years ago. From the point that they are dangerous and can start a fire, to the point where you can not disassemble and recycle the raw materials, how many will need to go to landfills, just like their fellow green energy producers, the windmill, which I will touch on shortly.

Electric car batteries are made from a number of minerals that are mined, mainly, you guessed it, in China. Most batteries are made from these 5 minerals: lithium, nickel, cobalt, manganese, and graphite. There are other various minerals needed depending on which battery is purchased. Here is what is needed to manufacture each EV battery. You must process 25,000 pounds of brine for lithium, 30,000 pounds of the ore for cobalt, 5,000 pounds of the ore for nickel, and 25,000 pounds of the ore for copper. Digging up 500,000 pounds of the earth's crust For just - one – battery. Read that again. Yes, look it up yourself, and most of these minerals are mined in China and now with child labor in the Congo! Wow! Why?

The above doesn't address how long a battery life is or what happens if there is a problem. As I said, a battery can not be recycled in most cases. It will go into a landfill, even though none of these yahoos that are trying to ram this stuff down our throats don't even realize that. These batteries and electric cars are supposed to be our saviors in regards to eliminating the use of fossil fuels, but there isn't even enough manufacturing power to build enough cars to supply not even 5% of the world's needs. So, how do these idiots think this will happen? Cars are needed, especially in North America, with all the urban sprawl that is occurring and the need for longer travel, whereas the EV can only really go about 300-400 km on a charge, and then, if you are lucky enough to find a charging station, you can spend the next 45 minutes to an hour for your vehicle to charge. People don't speak of the lack of infrastructure, but all they speak about is buying an EV, buying an EV. REALLY!

If you live in a populated, high-density area or one that doesn't have garages, have you thought of buying an electric vehicle? On top of that, have you ever wondered how you would charge that EV, especially when you don't have a garage to install the charging plug into? A lot of high-density cities don't have this type of space and infrastructure in their core, so what now, geniuses? Everyone is striving to convince you to buy into their long-term vision of a green New Deal and climate change, yet they don't understand what is needed to get there and what it will TRULY COST. No one is telling us the TRUTH? WHY?

So they are all worried about climate change, but they won't tell you that with all of these so-called initiatives, they are going to dramatically cut into the production of food for the world. They don't tell you this, so they don't scare you to change your vote. They have already started to do this by limiting the use of fertilizer, which is mandatory and necessary to grow any real amount of food that is needed in the world. This is because it's bad for our climate and our "survival"? In Canada, there is a big fight with the government, which is mandating a dramatic reduction in the use of fertilizer so WE can meet the goals we set for carbon emissions. A bunch of hypocrites who fly halfway across the world to attend a G7 and a G20 summit with their entire entourage, so they can enjoy the spoils of telling us all that we need to live within our means and with less, while these asses do what they want when they want. I guess again, they forgot about using ZOOM or TEAMs as a tool to accommodate all of these types of meetings and mitigate all of this unnecessary travel, but hey, you can get brown paper envelopes with lots of money over those ZOOM or TEAMS, now, can you? LOL. These can only be passed through to them in person, so let's fly to where it all takes place. So we are all going to have to use less food, in Canada at least, because we are contributing to climate change. They are going to stop or slow down the production of oil, which contributes to over 70% of Canada's GDP, because all of these morons think by doing this, they are going to save the planet. Little do they use their brains, as they don't appear to have any brains, that when they stop producing oil, other more vicious countries, with fewer restrictions, will pick up the slack, like Russia Iran and Venezuela to produce the oil that is needed to produce an unlimited amount of products that most of us are not even aware of that uses oil for manufacturing.

What a bunch of morons and deep thinkers. As I said earlier, you can't outthink someone who doesn't think!!! I love the saying that was taught to me a long time ago. No brains = NO COMMON SENSE. I really do think these people think they are all smarter than us, but you know what? They better look at history because the masses always win. As I said, change happens in only two ways, and history shows this. They are 1: REVOLUTION or 2: ASSISTINATION!! And change will happen because the masses will say, ENOUGH is ENOUGH, and take back what is rightfully ours, our EXISTENCE and LIVES!

So one of these geniuses just introduced an app that tracks the emissions of carbon dioxide, which we emit as humans. This inventor and pioneer of climate change, who has been flying in his private jet for over 25 years, thinks that he can sell something that shows governments how much carbon each individual emits by just breathing. Hmm, I wonder when the culling will start, just like it does with other species in this world when there are too many of that specific species. All people want to do is live a life that doesn't have all of these non-sensical restrictions that mean absolutely nothing, especially when all these restrictions come from and are established by a bunch of hypocrites that do the exact opposite of what they are insisting we all do. And then they don't have the decency to tell you that we can NOT live without Fossil fuels until we find a new non-emitting energy source. That is right, the human race, unless we want to live in tents, in the wilderness, or in a climate that doesn't have radical temperature changes, can not live without fossil fuels. Tell all Canadians in the winter to burn wood in their fireplaces, or tell all of these electric car people to plug in their electric cars into a plug with the use of a windmill as opposed to fossil fuels. It doesn't EXIST.

This is my final point on this topic, yet there are many more. Climate change will be the end of the human race, in my opinion, but not for the reason they are all talking about. It will be because all of these NON-COMMONSENSE thinkers will kill us all off because we will have a lack of food, fuel, heat, and anything else we depend on to maintain our existence. It won't be because we killed the planet. It will be because these idiots killed us and our way of life, which will probably drive us to kill each other. WAKE UP, PEOPLE, and start fighting back to this nonsense before it's too late. Make change happen, and not climate change, but the change to COMMON SENSE government that allows us to live our lives, to grow our own food, to drive our own cars that we choose to drive and not push us to the edge by scaring into taking us down a road of destruction. All of these people are either brainwashed or are being bought out because nothing they are selling makes sense. Why don't they tell you that 95% of all electricity is being produced by fossil fuels? Why don't they tell you that farmers can't grow enough food to feed us all without adequate fertilizer to grow this food? Why do they keep outsourcing all of the manufacturing to 3rd world countries and taking away all of our wealth? Ask them and see what their answers are. Asking them why they are destroying our way of life. Asking them what their end game is. Ask them why they keep flying in their private planes and staying in $5000 a night hotels powered by fossil fuels to discuss all of these changes amongst themselves while yearly increasing the money/taxes they steal from us.

The answer: WE HAVE NO COMMON SENSE, and we are trying to do something because we have no other way out because we are being forced into this agenda by people who have their own agenda!!

I will move on to the next topic, I think, which is important, but please remember, the above topic has many other aspects to it that many people have written an entire book on it. INFLATION is next, which is hurting us all yet is being manufactured by our brainless and non-common sense leaders.

9: INFLATION

Well, well, most of us who are reading this probably don't remember the good old '70s when house prices were in the 20-30k range, bread was 20 cents, and a bus ride was 25 cents, or maybe the '80s, when manufacturing was starting to really roll, and people started to make some real money. Houses ramped up over the 100k range for the first time, and bread was about a buck and a bus ride also about a buck, but remember, inflation stuck out its ugly head, and interest rates went up to 18-20%, but things were still somewhat affordable because the government didn't take as much from you. Then, there were the 90s when home and condo buildings went through the roof and boom again. 10 years later, we had inflation creep its ugly head, and rates went to 10-11 %, but things were still affordable to a degree. We had a bump in the 2000s when the worldwide net really started to be rolled out, with the handshaking 1200 or 2400 baud modem. Things got a little crazy in the 2000s because of greedy banks and business owners. They stole all of this money and made so many bad bank loans, which caused the entire banking system to hemorrhage. How greedy can some people be? Why doesn't anyone use Common sense anymore to treat their fellow human beings with decency and stop all of this craziness so we can all enjoy our daily lives? How much money do CEOs really need or deserve, especially the ones who didn't start the company? Those are the real crooks that conned their board of directors to pay them like they were gods of some sort.

Now, in 2022, we have true inflation, according to all of these oxygenertons, that barely know what day of the week it is after stealing all of our hard-earned money. Really? There is a big difference between this one and it's this. It's self-created by a bunch of morons in government office. Think about it. What causes inflation? They tell us too few products are being chased by too much money. Really you freakin idiots. Inflation is caused by a bunch of politicians printing too much money and handing it out like candy, free to everyone so they can spend it on frivolous items and making decisions that they are not educated to make. Why are you printing this money? All of a sudden, you think that you know what you are doing, or are you just trying to buy our votes? They tell us they know what they are doing, like the Bank of Canada governor or the Fed in the USA, but hey, if they knew what they were doing, why do we have inflation??

Inflation is another excuse to screw the middle class. In the bible, it was stated that usury rules are basically illegal. Here is the quote: "The Old Testament "condemns the practice of charging interest on a poor person because a loan should be an act of compassion and taking care of one's neighbor." In my personal opinion, and I do have a finance background, inflation is a way of screwing the middle class by taking more of their money without them realizing what each corrupt level of government is doing. So, a pandemic shows its ugly face, and every government in the world gives most of their citizens back some of their hard-earned money that they stole from them to begin with, driving up the government debts and deficits. They say that the pandemic and the lack of goods caused inflation. No, inflation is man-made because now it's time for all of these idiotic politicians to blame something else for their lack of doing anything. Let us deflect by causing prices to go up. If all of these geniuses were so smart, especially when they talk down to us, why has this happened and continues to happen?

We can do that by slowing down drilling for oil. 1st thing the new President did in the USA on their first day in office by canceling the Keystone pipeline. Then they tell you, no, that's not true, yet then they tell the truckers they can't drive their trucks by themselves unless they have a shot for COVID-19? Hmm, all the stars aligned for all of these countries, and now, low and behold, let's contribute to prolonging a war that means nothing, absolutely nothing, to the majority of the world. But all of these NATO governments are making it sound like it's vital we all contribute billions and billions of dollars to defend, you listening, "DEMOCRACY." What freakin democracy? Where is the money from one of the world's largest exporters of wheat? Exports of fertilizer? Why doesn't this country, which paid millions and millions to a president's son through alleged corruption, have no money and beg the entire world for financial and military support continuously without an end game? I will tell you why, so all of them can make excuses for stealing more of our money. It's called wealth re-distribution.   This is one of the main reasons that this so-called inflation was invented by genius politicians. Don't you think that some of those billions are going into the pockets of these world-corrupt politicians? Think about this, you Canadians. Did the Canadian Finance minister ever state her ties to the corrupt country of Ukraine? Have you ever heard her say anything about her past, her questionable past regarding Ukraine? No, and you will never hear that.

So we have inflation, man-made, and it's not going to stop anytime soon because every single world government is benefiting from it. Oh, forgot to tell you, the other beneficiary, the BANKS. Crooks and criminals, just like the mob, but they are " LEGIT," so they say. We now have to pay more for the money we borrowed? Think about it. You borrowed money for a mortgage and maybe a line of credit from a bank or credit union? Yet, they borrow it from the Bank of Canada and lend out your savings, yet when rates go up, why do your rates go up? Have you already borrowed that money? Ask yourself that. They lent you 100k, let's say, at 2.5%, and now you still owe them 100K because you refinanced and consolidated some debt, but now, you need to pay 6%? Why? Has the bank already lent you the money? Think about it, who is screwing who? Then, if you happen to have some money in a bank account, the bank is so nice they may pay you .25% interest. Wow, that's so nice of them, and then they lend this money out at 6%? Interest rates are made up? Who makes up interest rates? I will tell you who. It's the freakin people that don't read the BIBLE, that's who. Remember what I quoted from the bible about usury and the scam of interest rates? Interest rates are another way to steal money from hard-working citizens by the banks and government, like I said earlier, which are acting like the mob. Then they turn around and tell you, "We need to raise interest rates to slow down inflation and stop people from buying goods, but we will keep giving you money to buy these goods," instead of saying, "WE FUCKED UP," and we made a mess of the economy because we don't really know what we are doing, because in Canada our finance minister used to be a journalist, and knows nothing about finance'? Idiots and morons, all of them!!

Am I blowing your mind away? Because I know it's hard to think about these things, but I bet you, when you sit there and have a coffee with your buddies, you think it. Do you know why? Because you have COMMON SENSE, but all these assholes couldn't give a crap about you or me!!! All you want to do is go to work, pay your bills, live your life, and maybe enjoy a bit of a good life when you may possibly retire.

So take control of your life and your finances because no one else cares. You need to plan for your future and not rely on a bunch of liars in the government because all they care about is their positions, and most of them think they are entitled to these lifetime jobs and the crazy taxpayer-funded pensions and benefits that those positions come with. They travel the world on our dime and then are told not to because, as I stated earlier, YOU are contributing to CLIMATE change with your global trotting, and they are not. There is only one way to change these political entitlements. This is called setting term limits for all positions in elected government. Why aren't there term limits to these elected positions as there is for the world's most powerful position, the President of the USA? Do you know why? Because they figured we are all stupid, and hence the reason why they never had a real job and never really contributed to society in any real way! Most of these politicians, again, have never really done anything in life, and the few that have realized that they want a shot are eating at the trough as well, and hence when they get in, they realize that being in government is something only for the few that really know how to fuck the rest of the world, and are really good at lying and have mastered this skill!

Now, the Canadian government is complaining and looking into private company profits because they are stating that private companies are driving costs higher and hence creating and maintaining this inflation state we continue to be in. First off, what does the government know about private companies and creating jobs and wealth? Nothing, of course! Why does the government care about privately owned companies? Why don't they worry about creating jobs and bringing manufacturing back to North America, as opposed to doing absolutely nothing? This is something that can be done by cutting all of the red tape they created. Think about it, Canada; what has the Justin Trudeau government done for us in the last 6 years, aside from apologizing for issues from hundreds of years ago and writing cheques for reparations to all of these people from decades ago, to make themselves feel good? They have done absolutely nothing, and I challenge anyone to prove me wrong, and I will eat crow. All they have done is cater to human rights-violating countries, like China, who we rely on for our supply chain for EVERYTHING, and now they have PRINTED all of this money and created this man-made inflation that they keep shoving down our throats! But they keep blaming us, the citizens, for wanting to live our simple lives.

Inflation can be addressed in many ways, and one of them is to stop printing and spending money, Mr Prime Minister? Why don't you stop writing cheques to everyone except those who contribute the most to the social safety net? The government can really look at why inflation has gone in this direction and what they can do to minimize and reduce it. There is a very easy fix to this, and it's not by raising interest rates. It's by letting things play out, as people, we start to realize that we can't afford to spend anymore. Once people start spending their savings, and these savings start to shrink, the buying will slow down naturally. This new generation doesn't concern themselves with spending and debt because I believe what they realized during this pandemic is life is short, so live it and don't worry much about what the future holds. You will be taken care of by our social safety net that the minority is contributing to. This new generation has been so spoiled by the baby boomer generation that they really don't understand or realize what is currently happening, and they don't really seem to care because dad or mom will take care of it!

If the government doesn't do anything, what happens? Think about it. Probably nothing because prices will adjust accordingly. They don't want to address the bigger elephant in the room, which is gas prices, which in Canada appear to be pre-set and possibly are influenced by collusion. God forbid that the Canadian government looks into this price-fixing that we, normal people, know is happening. Prices in Canada seem to change Daily, and do you ever ask yourself why when most gas stations carry anywhere from 5-7 days worth of gas in their tanks? No one ever asks, but it's all about collusion and price gouging. This is the largest influencer and a contributing factor to inflation, yet no one in power wants to talk about it or address it in a more significant way by maybe building a gas refiner in this country that would contribute to lowering gas prices. This is being ignored because it would go against all of these idiots' ideological beliefs, contributing to CLIMATE Change. Living and gas is doing this. Really geniuses!!

Here is another example where the big brains in government don't work regarding why inflation happens and how to try to mitigate it. Excess money is a contributor, as anyone with any level of finance knows. So what the government is doing now in Canada is they are implementing a $ 10-a-day child care. Wow, these people don't learn, do they? So a family, let's say, has 2 kids, is currently paying anywhere from $100-$150 a day, and now they have applied to pay $10 a day. Where the heck do you they that difference is going to go now? Hmm, let's see, to possibly more excess spending? Does anyone ever think about this? There will be about $90-$140 dollars per kid on the low end. That will be excess money that a family will now have availed them to spend at their leisure and again add to this inflation the government is supposedly trying to rain in.   Hey, geniuses of the government, what do you think these people will be doing with it? Oh, if you don't know, let me tell you: they will be fueling the inflation you are currently trying to mitigate. The majority of people will spend this money on frivolous things, materialism fuels inflation, and now, with all of this newfound money that they have, interest rates will continue to go up until the government and all of those brainiacs realize they are the culprit that is fueling this craziness. COMMON-SENSE people, please use your brains. I am not the smartest person, but the only people whose rising interest rates are hurting are people who own homes and the other people who want to own homes. And the only people/corporations that are raising interest rates help are the "mafia" we call the banks. As I said, they take our money, do not pay any interest or small interest to us, charge us monthly fees, and lend out our money to others at much higher rates, not contributing at all to our GDP, as I said previously. These guys are a bunch of crooks, again, in my opinion. They are no better and probably worse than organized crime!

We have all levels of government trying to raise funds to cover their deficits now and blaming, guess what, Covid and the lockdowns. During COVID-19, did any level of government, which is Canada's largest employer, lay anyone off of their jobs? Answer: no way in hell. Hence contributing to inflation. All of them, from municipal, provincial, and federal levels, allowed all of their employees to work from home, even in cases where there was NO work to do from home because they couldn't access confidential files. The government doesn't tell us this, and yet they allow some employees to just collect paychecks for no work! They didn't lay off anyone, and keep paying their full salaries, and kept all of the services in place even if you couldn't access any services. Now we have the largest city in Canada, Toronto, and their mayor complaining and crying, stating they have a $1 billion dollar deficit, which they are having to fill because cities can not run a deficit by law. So what does this mayor do? He raised property taxes, another scam, by almost 7% to fill that gap, and he stated it's still below the rate of inflation. He blames the deficit on the lack of revenues because of Covid, but no one ever asks the hard questions, like, how many people, Mr Mayor, did you lay off during the pandemic? Why did you keep the transit system working almost at full service, yet you knew that there was less than 25% of the ridership, yet you kept providing full service and kept paying everyone their full salaries without any layoffs whatsoever? Now you are blaming Covid for your deficit, where you did nothing for 2 years of Covid to address the lack of revenue, and now you are crying to all other levels of government to contribute to filling this deficit hole for all your stupid pet projects all of your government morons feel you need. When are you going to be a responsible politician and take some accountability for your lack of actions that contributed to this deficit? Oh, I forgot, there is no such thing as a responsible and accountable politician because that's an oxymoron statement. They are all a bunch of liars and crooks and seem to forget there is only ONE taxpayer, and you can't keep going back to the well because, eventually, that well will dry up.

You wonder why there is inflation because every level of government wants to give everyone everything without figuring out a way to pay for it. They want to all keep spending and spending without any plans or accountability as to how to pay for it! We keep borrowing and spending for programs that are not necessary. Why don't you all live within your budgets, like we are expected to do? If you and I keep spending, they, the organized criminal banks, will repo our houses and all the possessions we own, but not the governments. Again, you don't have to because no one asks you a hard question, and no one holds you accountable. Inflation will always be used as a tool to strip each and every citizen of their hard-earned savings when every government in the world realizes that their citizens are inching closer to their independence, and then they will all try to reel us all in before it's too late. They will use every excuse in the book to steal from us because they feel they are entitled to their entitlements.

So, please, Mr. and Ms. government, next time we have inflation, just don't do anything. Oh, I forgot, you aren't doing anything except increasing interest rates, adding more profits to the corrupt banks, and stealing from the hard-working middle class. So, please stop pretending you know what you're talking about and leave it to the market to sort out.

Why don't you try doing something to address the next topic of drugs? Oh, I forgot, you tried this by legalizing cannabis and giving out free drug kits to drugged. How is that working out for you? Hmm, let's see. Next topic.

10: VICES: DRUG, ALCOHOL, AND BIG PHARMA

Since when did society change its stance on drugs? May they be soft or hard drugs? I am not sure when this started to happen because smoking pot has been going on for generations, but when did our politicians decide, on their own mind you, to legitimize and possibly legalize the use of drugs in our society, to the detriment of society as a whole, mind you, because all these politicians are idiots, or are they?

So, they all think we all do drugs, or maybe we should? Or maybe they want us all to do some type of drug so they, our political leaders, have better and more control over our lives. Have you ever watched the movie, "Boyz in the Hood?" The reason why I ask is this. If you did watch it, do you remember the scene when Laurence Fishburn brings his son, Cuba Gooding (Tre), and his friend Ricky and their friends to a corner, and he points to a billboard, which has ads for a liquor store sales and gun sales, and he says something like, "they put liquor stores in each corner, so we can drink and get drunk, so it dulls the pain? They also put gun stores everywhere so we can shoot each other so they can repress us all." Something like that. So, now, does it surprise you that they are legalizing Pot EVERYWHERE, all over North America, because all of these loser politicians have no solutions for their citizens, like maybe opening manufacturing plants in North America again or maybe bringing back jobs, or making the economy better, they want us all to smoke pot, and numb our existence. This is just the first step, and guess what happens next? This is going to make things better and bring you out of a poverty state. So they can keep stealing all the money we earn for their stupid pet projects. Let me name a few of these projects for these idiot, non-common sense politicians. In Canada alone, they, " the political geniuses," cut huge cheques and apologize for every past "Transgression" they feel they owe or committed 100-200 years ago. They buy pipelines and then give them away to Aboriginal people for free. They ship 100's of millions for non-sensical wars. They impose carbon taxes so they can steal more of your money. These are just a few things they want us all to feel numb to by smoking pot or even doing harder drugs that the Canadian government is trying to legalize. They are a bunch of Non-sensical idiotic politicians.

Instead of decriminalizing pot position, in Canada they legalized it. Why? Why not just let people smoke a little pot instead of legalizing it? Decriminalize it so kids don't receive records that stunt their employment and affect their future. No, The government thinks that by doing this, they can get more of our money from the already high taxes we pay instead of us buying it on the black market. Who does it affect? You know who it affects: all of the young kids who don't have a pot dealer right now. So they are introducing pot to a younger generation because the majority of people who currently smoke know someone who sells it and where to go to get some pot, or they know someone who can get it for them. So why are they doing this? This is a check mark for the box of " HEY, WE DID SOMETHING FOR YOU" politicians who do nothing each and every day but want to make it look like they do something. Think about this for a second before I move on. If you have ever worked a job, you usually work 8-9 hours a day, 5 days a week, but look at what a politician works. That's if they aren't traveling/flying on your dime somewhere pretending they are important. They may work 2-3 hours a day, maybe 3 days a week, considering they have a fully staffed office both in the capital and the riding they got elected in, who do the majority of the work and heavy lifting. All these politicians are figureheads, or should I say Bobbleheads, because that's all they do and how they act. They have no real plans or actions when they pretend they are on the campaign trail, trying to get elected to a position so they can loot it when they get there. All they are doing is lying to all of us.

Listen, I don't do drugs, but it really bothers me when I see about 10-12 pot stores open up in a small, maybe 5-mile radius in our small town. Why did some communities and politicians say no to having these places in their towns and cities but then vote yes to allow them? How the hell can there be that much business to be had when the prices are 30-40, maybe even 50% higher than the black market? Something really smells about this, and it ain't the pot. Why put more pot shops in Ontario than Tim's coffee shops? I am not sure what all of these idiot politicians are thinking, or sorry, forgot, they aren't thinking!!! Now, they are thinking of legalizing other drugs. People are dying hourly from overdoses, yet they want to legalize more drugs. They opened up places where you shoot things in your arm and even provided both the product and the needles. Are these idiots for real? WTF!!!. We spend millions and millions for outreach workers who are supposed to help these people because of all the taxes they take from us and tell us all it is for everyone so no one falls through the cracks or the mutual social net that is supposed to help all of us. Yet the only ones that our taxes are helping are the politicians and all of their buddies who are getting paid off. They can not provide good solutions for jobs and other ideas to benefit the greater good of society. And the sad part is, I have seen it with my own eyes and have seen the payoffs at these VIP parties that I happen to stumble into. Really!! No one cares, and no one gives a shit if you do drugs, kill yourself, and or do anything illegal, but don't you dare not pay your taxes, especially your property taxes, god forbid, because these fucks will take your house away because they are entitled, by whose laws? Their own laws because why do we pay property taxes? Look at that topic, and it will blow your mind. And if it does, sit down and spark a spliff!!! It will fix everything, and if it doesn't, no one freakin cares!!! Then go grab an overpriced bottle of liquor from the control board!!

These politicians keep inventing ways to oppress their citizens, no matter what type of excess they provide to their constituents. May it be drugs, cigarettes, or alcohol, they are all bad for us, but these fucks can't live without the tax money they collect, yet these vices are bad for all of us, yet they keep pretending its all good and keep raising the taxes on all of these vices! Why? What a bunch of hypocrites. They complain that the health system is stretched, but they keep pushing substance abuse throughout the country and keep legalizing things that will keep us stoned and oppressed!

DO ANY OF THESE ASSES HAVE ANY COMMON – SENSE!!!

I will leave you with this thought. If you drink or smoke or do drugs, do what makes you happy and be a good person, but we are all going to the same place. Dust to dust. Just remember. When all of these politicians start telling us all they are doing their best, call them on this crap!

In Canada, we legislate the distribution of Alcohol, especially in Ontario. Did you ever ask why we let this happen and not have an open market for the sale of Alcohol, like they do south of the border, where there is true free enterprise? Well, let me tell ya, COMMON SENSE, this doesn't exist, according to the politicians, because they can make all the money in the world knowing that you need to go through them to buy any alcohol. They raise prices as high as they want, and they pay crazy bonuses to executives of a monopoly, and they spend crazy advertising dollars to entice us to buy more of the things they say cause ill effects on our health system. If this isn't ass backward thinking, I don't know what is? I think they call that a monopoly, and that is, wait for it, against the law, yet we let the Ontario government have a monopoly on alcohol sales through the LCBO. WHY? WTF?

Why can't we privatize this? Why do we need to pay cashiers $30-40/hr to process orders, with crazy large pensions and other crazy salaries, for us, the people, to be able to buy a bottle of wine or spirits at 100% higher price or more, than crossing the border? Why has this occurred, and why can't it be changed? Because when you ask COMMON Sense questions, you know what the politicians tend to tell us, " THEY KNOW BETTER" for the greater good of the public. Why don't you all go F yourselves?

Now, as I stated, they want to legalize all types of drugs so they can deflect any accountability for their lack of any type of substantive actions toward improving our lives after they make all of these promises. I guess the only solution to this is to either accept it or leave it in a better place. I'm not sure if one exists, but if it does, I hope I find it soon.

The control over their citizens the Canadian and Ontario governments have is unmistakable: not a democracy as they state. It's more of a socialist society acting as a democracy, and if you ask any logical COMMON SENSE question, again, they will pretend that either they don't hear it or answer the question you didn't ask. Why legalize pot and other drugs and allow the private sector to sell them but keep control of the alcohol business? Hmm, doesn't it make you think that it's all about the green, that is, the cash they all make, either legally or illegally? What a bunch of HYPOCRITES!!

Don't these morons see all of the overdoses that are occurring all over the country? Do they ever ask why this is happening or what they can do about it? I am sure you know someone or know of someone who has overdosed because that person got in with the wrong crowd or couldn't handle the pressures of life all of these politicians put on us. Isn't it truly sad that people's lives are cut short, and they don't really get to experience all of the beauty that life has to offer because our political leaders will not do anything about the illegal drugs, or maybe now legal drugs, that are killing people?

All of these safety nets we speak of don't exist, and now, as I stated, the government wants to legalize other drugs. Why, why, in God's name, don't any of these idiots do something right? Stop legalizing drugs, and do your freakin job. Oh, I forgot, you need common sense to do something right, like your job, Mr.Lifetime Politician.

Now, these genius politicians have legalized sports books in Ontario specifically, which they were adamant about not doing just a few years ago. I wonder why these politicians agreed to do this. Wonder if any of them have personally benefitted by legalizing sports betting. In Ontario, they had pro-line, yet they banned the NBA. Now, you can bet on anything you want, and it's ok. With the advent of legalizing pot and now legalizing sports betting, do these politicians ever think that this may lead to more social issues? Probably, but they may think that providing access to these is a way of making us forget about the more important issues they aren't addressing, such as the highest taxed jurisdictions in the world and the continuous raising of these taxes, because politicians, can control their spending and are addicted to tax dollars like they are making their citizens, addicted to pot and gambling. Like they did when they didn't ban cigarettes, but keep raising taxes on them, so they can keep stealing your money and not telling you they are bad for you. Common-sense people, Don't be as stupid as your politicians!!! Cigarettes and their continued availability brings me to this topic.

Have you ever thought about the bad things in life, like cancer, which, more than likely, has affected almost everyone in one way or another? You think, boy, if only there was a cure? Or why isn't there a cure, especially with all the technology we have to address it? We have AI, self-driving cars, facial recognition, and a bunch of other crazy things that you dreamt of growing up but now are reality, yet we can't cure cancer. Do you ever think that " they " don't want to cure cancer because it creates so much wealth in this world? Yes, I said something that most of us only think of but are scared to say because we are scared to say the truth. I really believe there is a cure, and if there isn't, they are trying hard enough, especially with all the money they ask us to contribute each and every month to the cause. There are lotteries, runs to find the cure, raffles, sports teams contributing, the pink ribbon campaign, and a lot more that could cover a whole book on the topic of functions that collect all of this money, with no cure or no announcements of a potential cure. It's 2023; why or how is this possible? We have sent rovers to Mars and people to the moon, yet we can't find a cure for one of the most deadly diseases on this planet that affects us all. We found a vax for COVID-19, or DID WE? In only a few months? But we can't find a cure for cancer with all of the billions of dollars every year that are thrown in that direction?

I will leave this with the following: maybe BIG PHARMA doesn't think it's profitable to find this cure.

Well, I think I have COMMON-SENSE like the majority of you do, and I am sure you think the same way. It's business, and that's all that matters. If they want to release the cure, they could do that any time, in my opinion. Wake up, people, stop contributing to this nonsense. They keep asking for cancer money to find a cure, yet year in and year out, there seems to be NO CURE. Why don't you ask your politicians next time if they want to comment on this topic?

Drugs are invented each and every day. How safe they are is another topic for discussion. Do you ever watch a commercial on TV that is promoting a new drug, and you watch it and think, why are the side effects 2-3 times longer in the ad than what the drug is meant to cure or address? If it was so safe, why do they need to tell us of the 100's side effects? Did they not test this drug, and wasn't it approved by the drug agency? Don't use these drugs, people. Use some COMMON-SENSE. They don't work, and if they did, they wouldn't need to pay big bucks on national TV ads to entice you to try them. Why would you do this unless you were desperate and looking for anything to help you? Is anyone held accountable for these new drugs, as most of them don't really work? But these BIG PHARMA companies are making billions of dollars for creating a drug that may or may not work, but they are convinced it is, so they spend millions to advertise it. They did this with the COVID-19 VAX, and no one is being held accountable for all of the " supposed deaths" that the VAX caused. COMMON SENSE, people, please use it unless you really have to and have no alternative. Look up the stats for all these new drugs, and you will see that the majority of them don't really work as a cure, but they numb the symptoms, so you can possibly live a somewhat better life with all of these side effects. Good luck with that, as we are all getting older and will need more drugs to survive, so I feel sorry for all of us because of all these greedy BIG PHARMA assholes. They are never, ever honest with you unless they get caught on a hot mic, just like the COVID-19 vax executives, who basically said the vax didn't really work like they promised it would. NO ACCOUNTABILITY for these assholes either, just like your politicians!

Why were pharma companies invented? Can anyone answer this question, or does anyone remember the reasons this happened? They were NOT invented or started to make things worse for the population but to make things such as life easier and more comfortable. So why has this pandemic caused such consternation with these companies? It appears that they are becoming greedy, trying to create and sell vaccines, that in a lot of people's judgments, don't do what is promised of them. Since when did any of these Pharma executives put profit ahead of decency and COMMON-SENSE? I guess we all know what the end game is for all of these executives, don't tell the truth about your company, spread as much vaccine as possible, make billions of dollars on the back of the worlds taxpayer, and don't give a crap about the ramifications, because before you know it, we are all going to die, and no one in power will give a shit!!!. Why are these Pharma executives allowed to get away with all of these non-truths and are not held accountable for anything?- The only possible answer is there are no oversight committees or people overviewing them, and if there are, then they are all in bed together and being given brown paper bags to look the other way!! Let's face it: COMMON-SENSE, morality, and decency were thrown out the window with most of these companies, and it appears that they may be in bed with creating even further viruses to propagate these vaccines even into the future. But you need to ask yourself, why? But again, none of these jackasses will ever answer this because all they care about is themselves and their profits and stock options. Really people!!! Have you all forgotten about human decency and the human race!!! You should all be ashamed of yourselves and just go to hell, where you belong.

I just reviewed all the vices that make the world go round, the politicians that take advantage of us, and the taxes they are addicted to. One last thing I want to add here: in my opinion, this new legalization of drugs and even gambling will be the downfall of the Western world as we know it. But I hope I am wrong, and only time will tell, but I don't think I am with all of the craziness that is happening all around us. We all need to keep asking our politicians why they keep doing stupid things and ask them to write an accountability statement so if and when they do the next stupid thing, we can hold them accountable and get rid of their asses and their gold-plated pensions. Ask them, go ahead!

Net topic, if you survive, Mid-Life crisis and the ups and downs of it. Then, we will take the final hurdle in life's journey: Retirement!!! LOL.

11: MID-LIFE (CRISIS)

Why do so many people, usually men, go through something that is referred to as a mid-life crisis? I am a man, and I never really had this experience or issue, not yet anyway, but I am not sure how to refer to it, sorry. We all try to live our lives, for the most part, in a positive way, and we try not to do the wrong thing. If you are so lucky or fortunate to have a good life, you know what I mean. Notice how I stated that negative position and not positive position for a reason. We try to live our lives trying to do the right thing. ? Lol. Or so we think we try to? We grow up, hopefully, raised by caring parents and then go to school. Most of us get a job, and if we want, get married and try to have a family if that is what we want. The world is now ever-changing, and things may not progress in this type of order any longer if you are reading the news lately.

You do all the right things, as I mentioned, and then, BOOM, one day, it hits you. What hits you is the question? I really don't know, but something does. It's not COMMON-SENSE that hits you, but I believe the opposite. From what I see and what I have been told, you want to throw everything away and do the exact opposite of what you have been doing for the last 30-40-50 years. You want to reignite that lost youth possibly, or maybe relive the regrets that you didn't experience. I really don't know what or why.

Some of them want to buy a sports car. Some of them want to travel the world by themselves. Some of them want to quit their jobs and live on the beach. And then, there are those who want to leave their families and shack up with a hot model 30 years younger than them. WHY? Listen, I am not here to judge or preach about this topic, as I have never experienced this, but why would you want to throw away everything you worked so hard for just because let's face it, you can't handle what you are going through currently in your life, but you and everyone else calls it "A mid-life crisis', really? What triggers this? I am not a psychologist or psychiatrist, but I do know life isn't always easy. But if you are fortunate enough to live a good one, why throw it all away? Why don't they call it what it really is? People, and many men, tend to give up on life a lot easier than women. Males usually give up on everyday life quicker, and you want to move into a fantasy world! Use some common sense, people and men, and don't throw away everything. JUST TAKE A BREAK! Take the time you need to regenerate and take a step back. You know you can do that. Take some time off if you have the assets to do that that is. But don't give up. Like I tell all the people that I know that ask me: "STAY IN YOUR LANE." It's not worth it. Veering off to some no-good place will always get you into trouble, and there is no good way back, usually.

Go buy a sports car! Go Travel! or even go get a hairpiece if that will make you happy and more confident in yourself! Go do what you have to do! Ask your spouse for a Hall pass if you want. Watch the movie, it's not bad, but it's not for everyone! And for those who don't know what that is, watch the movie Hall Pass, and you will figure it out. It's not really worth it, but if that's what it takes to save your situation, family, marriage, job, or career, do it because throwing everything away is not worth going through a mental breakdown and then realizing, albeit too late, that you made a mistake, I know the last couple of years, 2020-2022 specifically, have been hard for all of us, going through this crazy virus, that we still don't know anything about, but, take a break and try to save yourself and your family! Many of us can and maybe don't even understand why our bodies and minds have changed, but it has been because of our lack of human interaction, and this has really impacted most of us from a social perspective, as humans are mainly social beings.

I take it that it happens to the other gender as well. I know a number of women who want to do a few things, also. As I said, some want to spend a lot of money on things like shoes and purses, and then there are some who want to have a secret fling for no other reason but maybe to spice things up in their lives. A number of women want to make themselves look younger, and I mean a lot younger, without really completely understanding what the ramifications are of these types of procedures. Some go well, some not so well, and I mean really not so well, and some even regret these types of procedures and surgeries. They never really leave their families because I think men forgive easier than women do. I am not really sure why, but we do, in my opinion, because we see things in black and white, and it's usually easier and more comfortable to stay where we are instead of trying to start completely over. I don't call that COMMON-SENSE, but some would. Guys, as we know, see things as black and white, not in color. We seem to think this way so as to make our lives easier. Both genders are built differently, as we know, hence the different reactions to the hard paths in life. We do things differently and react to things much differently, so there is no real reason to try to figure this out except to accept it and move on.

I really didn't want to approach this topic lightly, but let's face it: if you haven't gone through this part of your life, good for you. I am not only surprised you are reading this book, but you will go through this, so please do the right thing and don't put others through it with you. If you need to do this thing, do something that doesn't affect your family life. Don't throw everything you worked so hard to build away in a flash. Take the time you need for yourself and make the right decisions. Go buy a car, go on a trip, or do something that will not put your family on a roller coaster that will never stop at the right level. Enjoy your life and your family. You can do both at the same time. It really is worth it.

Common sense certainly doesn't prevail at this time in your life, but if you think before you jump, you will probably save yourself and your family at this stage of your life a lot of heartache and headache and a lot of legal fees, LOL. I have always wanted to do a lot of things at this stage of my life aside from working 50-60 hours a week to pay the bills and provide for my family, but when my mind goes off to this place, I always think about my father, who always taught me about how important family is, and to do everything you can to provide for your family, put them first, ahead of your wants, and do the right thing. Always do the right thing because it will pay you tenfold in the future and in your next life. A lot of people may disagree with this, but being selfish isn't how you should live.

The number of times I would travel for business and see colleagues do things that I would shake my head at, but a small part, a very small part of me, would think, wow, must be nice to stray outside your lane, but then I would know what the right thing to do is, and I remove myself from that situation, head back to my hotel room, and do the right thing. I would see this almost on a regular basis, and watching all these episodes made me not want to travel for business any longer. I never told anyone this, but like I said, I always ' STAYED IN MY LANE", like it or not, because I love my life and my family, and I will never, and I mean never, do anything to jeopardize that. A lot of people take family for granted until it's too late. Please, people, use some COMMON SENSE and don't do stupid things. Use the brain you were given, and don't use excuses, like alcohol or drugs, which have been legalized in all parts of North America, without understanding the ramifications, which are more prevalent, to justify doing these stupid things.

Going for a drink with your co-workers after working hours, especially if they are female co-workers that are involved, doesn't end very well, sometimes, so don't put yourself in that position. I have seen enough of these situations in my professional life to think, why do people do these things? Why do people need to tell you everything that is going WRONG in their lives at these events? Do you not think that we all have daily issues we deal with? Some of us have better coping skills than others, but some people need to tell you about everything that is wrong with life, especially their personal life. They can, for some reason, not appreciate the good things in their lives. I am not sure if this is for empathy or to justify something they are probably doing wrong or thinking of doing, to see what the reaction of others would be. Listen, people, suck it up, don't think of yourself first, and there is no reason to discuss your dirty laundry with others to see if others want to share theirs, or worse, want them to justify the stupid mistakes you have made. Midlife creeps up on all of us, some sooner than others, but the sooner you realize what it is, the sooner you will make the right choices and do the right thing. Use your common sense to be a good person.

Remember, if you don't put yourselves in awkward situations during this time in your life, you won't have to make these types of decisions or choices. Use some common sense, and do the right thing. Please, for yourself and your family, act like a responsible adult because they deserve it. There are a lot of reasons why the above happens, and there has been a lot of money and time spent analyzing this topic by a lot of professionals. Especially after the pandemic and people reassessing their priorities in life, a lot of people made drastic changes that they now truly regret. I have been told that people nowadays have more time and more access to things, like the internet, that allows them to explore options that the past generation never had. Going into these holes will do a lot of damage because these places will let you fantasize about things and will bring trouble to your real world. In the past, people went to work, came home, had dinner, watched some TV, possibly went out, and then did it all over again. They enjoyed spending quality time with their families. Now, we have this www thing they call the internet that is really creating a generation of people that can explore and experience things that are instantly gratifying, which will cause you issues.

Again, think before you jump, COMMON-SENSE, and it will bring you more satisfaction and long-term enjoyment than being spontaneous and reckless. Men and women have similar goals in life, believe it or not, that is to have a nice life, a successful career, and possibly a great family with a significant spouse. This is true, no matter what this crazy media is telling us each and every day. So enjoy these great things that we all work so hard to build and strive to get better as a human race.

Now let's move on to the last and, in my opinion, the most important topic in this book. The end of your working life, that is, if it's in your cards. If you are lucky enough to get to this point in life, after all of the craziness and things in this world that we work so hard in, you need to be prepared and plan for RETIREMENT. If you don't plan, either sooner or later, you may regret it because you still need money to live your life, even after you finish working full time. That's if you want to have any real kind of retirement above and beyond just waiting for that retirement cheque from the government. LOL

12: RETIREMENT:

If you are reading this and if you have kids or are planning on having them, PLEASE, PLEASE, teach your kids the importance of saving and to start saving, even a little, very early in life. You will not regret it if you do, and you will definitely appreciate it. Maybe not for retirement, but save some money, each and every paycheck you get, for some future purchase or even for a little rainy day fund. This will set them up for future success when everyone else may be struggling. They will have something to fall back on when they need to, and we all need to, once or twice in life. Use some COMMON SENSE, parents, and teach your kids a little, just a fraction, about saving for the future. Finance 101 is necessary and should be mandatory for all of us, starting from a young age, so we aren't dependent on the state to support us.

When you start in the real world, you get a job, many jobs, probably, and you save a bit, and you spend a lot, and all you hear on TV is, "Are you saving enough for retirement?" You hear all of those ads about ROI, what the hell is ROI, and why should l care, what does that mean, and how does that matter right now? You keep trying to save, but it's pretty hard, too, because you want to enjoy living and doing things with your friends and co-workers, and then you meet someone and start dating, and BOOM, you talk about getting married and realize that you don't really have enough money because you didn't save enough. LOL. You get married and need to find a new place to live, and there are a lot more expenses, and even though there are now two incomes, it appears there is less money to spend and SAVE. Oh, oh, the money is no longer as plentiful as it was when you were single and in total control.

You think, what the hell is going on? Maybe I should have listened to someone about all of those ROI ads that told me they could help me save for retirement because they say I am going to need, like, a couple of million dollars to retire. Crap, I only make $70, 80, 90k per year, so how am I going to say a couple of million dollars. Wow, now this is quite depressing because retirement seems so far away, but believe me, time flies, and life keeps moving, and before you know it, here comes RETIREMENT.

You seek out a financial professional to help you determine the path you need to be on to start saving for all of those big events that will now enter your life after marriage, such as buying a home, buying a new car, having kids, and possibly trying to enjoy some vacation and travel. They start telling you that you need to put more money away each and every paycheck, and you wonder how you can do that, but believe me, if you take their advice, you will be way better off because YOU CAN DO IT!

Well, let me explain something to you about compound interest and savings. If you save $50 per week for 40 years, and you start working at age 20, then your principal savings will be $104,000, but if you invest it at a 5% annual return, you will have about $300,000 at the end of that time frame. That may not sound like a lot, but all of it adds up to a couple of cups of coffee per day. This small amount will not really put you out, and you won't even notice it. Please try to do this and avoid those expensive lattes each and every day. You will be able to enjoy more than lattes at the end of the journey. Don't get me wrong, enjoy a latte once in a while, but put the rest into savings. Wish someone taught me this when I was young and starting my working life. COMMON SENSE people work in a big way when it comes to saving for RETIREMENT.

Another aspect that you definitely need to take advantage of, if you are fortunate enough to be in this position, is to take advantage of any savings program your company may have to offer you. In Canada, it's usually called a DCPP, defined contribution pension plan, and is something a lot of people ignore because they may feel that either they won't be at the company that long or it takes away from their take-home pay. Well, let me inform you of what this is. The company will take pretax dollars, which are about 25-30% more than after-tax dollars, and will provide some sort of top-off from their end. Say you make $50k per year, and you opt into a 10% contribution, and the company gives a 5% or 50% contribution; then this is what happens. That's $1k per week, or $100 contribution you make, and the company will make an additional $50 per week contribution on your behalf. Over 40 years, this will provide you with a return of approximately $903,000, using a 5% return. And imagine if your annual return is more than 5%, let's say 7%, which works out to be $1.5 MILLION. Isn't that crazy from just very small savings at your work? You know what your weekly net paycheck will turn out to be. Instead of making $650/week, you will receive about $600/week, depending on the tax rate. But look at the return, and with your annual raises, you may well be a lot higher than that at the end of it all. I am not a financial advisor or planner, but I want to tell you this: PLEASE START SAVING, even if it's a little bit because you will be way better off in the long run and won't have to count on any government support when it's all over. And the other thing you will do is give your next generation a head start when they inherit your life's hard work.

Remember what I said a lot earlier: every single responsible parent wants to make life better and easier for their kids. It may sound difficult, but it really isn't, and you never see it until you need it! And SURPRISE, it's there for you, all that hard work. If they don't, they are definitely not responsible or good parents, in my opinion. The great part of this type of savings is you can always take it with you from job to job. This money is always yours. Yes, these savings with your company are always yours, so don't think that you will forfeit it or leave it behind if you leave that company or organization. Use some COMMON-SENSE, and enroll in that DCPP when you can and as soon as you can, and don't give it a second thought.

Let's talk a little about retirement from a different perspective, which is about living life along the way. Yes, I said it: make sure you enjoy your life on this journey, because remember, it's not about retirement, but what you do on the path to retirement and all the great things this world has to offer us all. What do I mean by that? Well, there is a lot of life to live, like going out to dinner, buying yourself and your family special presents, going on vacations, and enjoying the world. There is more to this world than the place you currently live in, so go explore it, as it will benefit you emotionally and spiritually, believe me. These things and more are things you need to keep in the forefront because before you know it, you go from 25 to 50 years old, and you will look in the mirror and be shocked to realize as I did, WTF, what happened to me and my life and goals that I had. Let me tell you from experience it goes fast, very fast, so you can either get on that road of life or stay on the sidelines and miss it all. Getting on the road is a vastly better journey, and don't let these negative people affect your decision to enjoy your life.

I know we live in an ever-changing world that more people find scary, but if you don't enjoy it and live it and be the focus of your life, then you will REGRET it. I do very much want you to open your eyes and not REGRET the precious life that you were given and that you did not enjoy along the way. Again, you will wake up, and you may or may not realize what you did or did not do because maybe you were scared of the world, you didn't have enough money, or you were scared to lose your job. Well, let me tell you, DON'T BE SCARED of living your life. We are all blessed if you are reading this, but we need to make sure we understand how precious life is and it should be enjoyed and lived. I know these are all cliches, but if you ask anyone who is older than you, they will tell you the same thing: go live it and enjoy it all because before you know it, you may not be able to, physically or mentally, it all creeps up on you.

Retirement comes up quickly for you. Most of us are really busy with life, trying to juggle all aspects, to our amazement, between work, family, activities, and all other things. BOOM, you are maybe in your late 50s and say to yourself, What happened? You realize you are on the downslope side of the pendulum, and then you have or you already did have a mid-life crisis. (one of the previous chapters, if you recall). You had to buy that sports car, go get fake hair, or possibly have a fling with some young thing, which you realize later was REALLY STUPID, and you will probably regret it. We all do a lot of things on the journey, and some we are very proud of, and some we really really regret and probably want to forget. We should have used some COMMON SENSE on the journey instead of just being stupid. Not thinking of ramifications is a big mistake when you do something that may be considered questionable. But again, if you think it's a good thing, maybe try it, as long as it doesn't negatively affect you or your family. Experience it, especially if it's something you want to do, BUT always use some COMMON-SENSE, as we were all given it, but some refuse to use it at times.

So you want to start making plans to retire, but you still have a couple of kids, one just starting university and the other one just finishing high school. You know you don't want to spend the rest of your life in a winter wonderland. You really don't want to spend your remaining years, maybe 5, 10, or 15, but maybe not too many beyond that because you start questioning your mortality.

You sit down at the kitchen table to try to figure it out. All the information your parents graced you with about how to be fiscally responsible on this journey. The save a little each paycheck thing, the save in the DCPP thing, the save in the RRSP thing, and maybe a little more in some other places you socked away. Maybe you were fortunate enough to buy some real estate or even a cottage or vacation home. You grab the stack of papers and the laptop and start typing all of the information into the spreadsheets. You are scratching your head every few minutes, trying to figure out what you are looking at. You look at the numbers on each piece of paper, and every time you enter a figure in the spreadsheet, it brings a smile to your face. You keep going and keep looking at the clock. Boy, there are a lot of papers on the table, you think. Keystroke after keystroke, you are getting close to the end, with a little nervousness in your bones. Have you done enough? Have you followed your COMMON-SENSE approach to life and saving for the best part? Have you followed all the advice given to you along the way? You have some savings, you have an RRSP, you have a TSFA, you have a DCPP, and you are blessed enough to have a DBP also, with your largest nest egg being your home equity. You keep pressing the enter key and the shift 8 key, and then you are finally finished. Thank goodness. You really don't want to look at the totals yet, so you stand up so as to prepare yourself emotionally. It is emotional, even if some people don't think so, your mortality. How did you do along the journey and the many roads, twists and turns, ups and downs?

Viola, you see the number at the bottom of the screen. You see this number, in your opinion, you do a double look, and then you say it internally.

$1,752,344.41. Not including your home equity. Because you still have to live somewhere? You look again and then ask yourself, "IS IT ENOUGH TO RETIRE?" Is it enough to keep your 2 kids in school until they want to enter adult life, or do they want to keep educating themselves indefinitely? But does it really matter? It's up to them and what they want to do, not you. This is a new generation. You haven't told your spouse yet as to what you were doing and why you were doing it. You were thinking that the numbers were going to be different, and you wouldn't have to have this conversation as of yet. But, you are both shocked and pleasantly surprised at the results and totals and now you know, in your mind, that you need to have that discussion with your spouse. The one about the next phase of your life. The most important and significant person in your life, next to the one that gave you life. You will need to give her your vision, see what her vision is, and see if there is a mutually happy place for both of you to meet. Maybe your spouse has other ideas that they haven't talked about with you as of yet. You start playing that conversation in your head over and over again. How do you approach it? What are the first words that come out to set the table and the conversation in the right direction? You have been at your job for a very long time or many different jobs, but it's been a long, long time, and you have spoken to a number of high-level executives, and you shouldn't have an issue in having this type of difficult conversation. You are a professional, and now you have to have this life conversation with your significant other. You grab some water and say, yes, this is the time. I will lay all the cards on the table and basically state that " I HAVE HAD ENOUGH " of the day-to-day grind, and I think we need to move to the next phase of our lives so we can enjoy the remaining time we have on this earth, while we both have our health, both physical and mental health, as you may already know, you need both to keep enjoying the journey. We need to see and do things that we have spoken about but have never gotten around to seeing or doing because there is plenty left on the bucket list. We need to experience the joys and the amazements on this planet we just keep talking about and haven't been able to experience. We need to get rid of all the extra stuff we have purchased that was necessary but is no longer needed and is taking up space just because it is. The last thing on your mind, until it comes to you, is, " What if she says I am crazy, and you still have a lot of work left in you." What then? Let's see what happens, but COMMON-SENSE will prevail, probably, and it will all work out. I am pretty sure of that!

Retirement is both joyous and scary at the same time. Which path do you travel now? Which road do you take.? It's something that has to be discussed, and a decision will need to be made. Is it the correct one? Only time will tell. But at least we have $1.75 million. Yes, we are millionaires. It might not be a lot of money to some people, but it is to you, and we worked hard to make it and hard to save it. What's our next move?? Let's figure it out together, and only time will tell. We used a lot of COMMON SENSE on this journey to get where we are now, and if you do get to this stage, you should be very proud of it and what you accomplished. A lot of people never really make it and have to keep working well beyond where they should be because either no one educated them early or they may have had a lot of other difficult challenges in life that they couldn't handle. But you did. You went the extra mile, and you made all of the right decisions, which some people call sacrifices. You deserve it because you made it happen with all of the COMMON-SENSE decisions you made on this journey.

Before I close this chapter, I want to talk briefly about ROI again and the stock market. I learned a long time ago from a very well-known stock trader that if you don't have the stomach for it, don't play the stock market unless you educate yourself and leave your emotions at the door if you do. I educated myself in this area, and with all the meetings and research I did, the same phrase was always mentioned to me. Here it is: "Markets don't just move, they are moved"! What does this mean? It means you are a very, very small fish in a big ocean, and your couple of thousand dollars will not make a bit of difference when you buy a stock. If you move away from Mutual funds and buy stocks, remember this: do your homework, and use some COMMON-SENSE. Do take a tip from a friend, as they don't know any more than you do. If you take a tip or hear something, make sure it's from a professional, and even then, do your homework, or you will probably lose most, if not all, of your investment and become very emotional and make bad judgment calls. Again, use COMMON-SENSE, and you will be way ahead.

I will leave off with this on retirement, as I have had a lot of family loss over the past years. A number of close relatives have passed, and they never did anything with their lives. They never experienced different countries, different cultures, or anything unique from other people. They were always worried about retirement and having enough when they did. Most of them were well off, and they did well for themselves and their families, yet they thought, enough is not enough. They kept putting even more away and kept working when they should have made the decision to start living because they worked hard enough to get to the end of the first part of their lives. Let me tell you something. When you have a good work and family ethic, something or someone always looks after you, and you will be okay. There is a higher power out there that takes care of us all, believe it or not. So why am I writing this? It is to remind people to enjoy the journey before it's too late. There is a lot of life to live and a lot of things to experience, so don't be scared to go experience life because you worry about the last parts of it. Again, the last parts of your life are not that enjoyable, as most of us will be disabled in some form or another and will have to rely on others to assist us, so what good will it be then to have all of this money and wealth in the bank, and then sit and think about what might have been or could have been, as the saying goes. Don't let life creep up on you and take it away from you before you have the chance to experience the fantastic and great things this world has to offer us because we have been blessed with what our previous generation left us or what we earned on our own. Please don't let life live you; live it, as it's worth every minute of it. Don't be a bystander but a participant. Some may have less, and some may have more, but one thing we all have is the opportunity to enjoy and experience the journey that's called life. Use your COMMON-SENSE, and don't let others tell you what you can or can't do because they think they are smarter than you are. You are a smart person, and don't let anyone tell you otherwise as if they do, then you are the one that will be worse off.

The last thing I will say about this RETIREMENT PORTION is, please plan, even if it's a little because it will all be worth it when it's time to enjoy it!

Again, go live life, as it is definitely worth living.

SUMMARY AND LAST THOUGHTS?

COMMON SENSE THOUGHTS THAT IS!!!

As you have seen over the chapters, there are a lot of things that have occurred and are still happening in our lives that don't make any sense, yet we are supposed to believe that it all is supposed to be benefitting us. From politicians to simple people that you meet, everyone thinks that it all makes sense to them. If that is the case, then none of them have any COMMON-SENSE.

You are born into this world, lucky, in a 1st world country with all the opportunities that are availed to all its citizens. You go through life, hopefully being raised by responsible and caring parents and possibly siblings. You grow and experience all the gifts that life has to offer, from family outings to meeting different people and hopefully making friends. Then, as a growing adolescent, you start realizing that people don't think or act like you. You walk on the right side of the street. You do what you were taught, all the right things that your parents enforced into you as the right ethics and morals, and what for this, they say to you, THESE ARE ALL COMMON-SENSE things that all people do, each and every day.

We grow up, hopefully, to become adults and pursue something as an occupation that would make us happy because all you hear growing up is to do something you love because it will never feel like work. I think I mentioned that previously, but you know what? Even though that statement seems like a COMMON SENSICAL statement, it's very rare that anyone, maybe 1% of the population, finds that, but it should be easy to do, shouldn't it? Hmm, wish it was that easy.

We start to meet people, and they do things, again, that aren't or don't seem normal to you because you were raised to use your brain and think and do things that seem to you as common sense. So why do so many people act and do things that do seem right?

I mention this throughout the book. How do we make things right? I really don't know because there are so many variables in our lives that we can not control, even though we should be able to. I mentioned things like taxes, governments (democracies? Ya right), drugs, wars, and other nonsensical things that should be happening, and if they do, the people who created them should use some COMMON SENSE to make them as mainstream as possible.

I wrote this book because every single day of my adult life, nothing makes sense, from the amount of taxes we pay to the fact we can not buy alcohol at a decent price because of the monopoly to all the drugs people do to numb the pain from the daily life that they can't handle. Why does all of this happen, and why does none of it make any sense? Why doesn't anyone who has any power or control, above and beyond your control, do nothing at all to help anyone in a substantial way? They keep taking our money, which they call taxes. They keep raising these taxes and keep saying you still need to pay more. Why, or please tell me why? When is enough, enough? From personal taxes from your paychecks to property taxes that allow you to rent your own home that you will never own to consumption taxes that all keep going up, when does it end? Don't say it, but yes, that seems to be the answer to these questions. There is only one end to all of this NONSENSE! You want to change it, but you know you can't because if you do something, like start a petition, and tell all your towns population to sign the petition not to pay their property taxes unless they start coming down, they are all scared that these moron politicians and monopolized banks in Canada, will foreclose on all of the houses. This is the only way that things change or can be changed.

I have always said this and truly believe, deep in my heart, that there are only two ways to make change in this world, and history proves this. The two ways are 1: Revolution and 2: Assassination. Check all the history books or the web, and this is 100% true. These are the only two ways to make change. If we want to make a change, we in the first world can only think of Revolution, and that really means protests, petitions, and making hard stances, like not paying taxes and giving the middle fingers to all levels of government until they start using some COMMON-SENSE in their policies and things they do to help their citizens.

Summary

We tackled a lot of topics above. I really wonder how many you can relate to and how many really get your goat, as the expression goes. Many of you can relate to them and the common sense or lack thereof, hence the reason for our daily frustrations in life. We try to go through life, the highs and lows, and everything in between, but when we really get going, we ponder the question:

Do these people really have Common-sense or are they all just stupid? I really hate that word, but I needed to use it to emphasize what I was trying to write.

I hope you enjoyed this, laughed somewhat, and maybe even shook your head in agreement with some of the examples I spoke of, as we can all relate to some of these topics.

Now go enjoy your and life, live every day with common sense, useless you want to laugh, that is!!!!

Providing for your family: Common Sense

Paying Taxes: Not so much

Going to Work: Common Sense

Sleeping in – Not so much

Paying your bills: Common Sense

Being an ethical and moral person: Common Sense

Just doing the right thing: Common Sense.

Driving on the wrong side of the road: STUPID

Ripping people off STUPID

Crime of any kind: STUPID

EPILOGUE

As we conclude this journey through the complex yet thrilling maze of life, we find ourselves reflecting on the common-sense thoughts that have guided us. The world is filled with contradictions, absurdities, and nonsensical occurrences; what keeps us afloat in the vast ocean of chaos are the values and principles that have been instilled in us since childhood.

Life is never a linear path, and it shouldn't be. What would be fun in that, huh? Throughout this book, we've explored the perplexities of different aspects of life. Those aspects are the threads woven into the very fabric of our lives. They challenge our understanding and often leave us questioning the sanity of the world around us. But through this series of highs and lows, don't forget that there are countless doors on the way. If one closes, the other opens, and the life goes on. We may meet people who amaze us with their choices and actions, something beyond comprehension. But amidst it all, always seek the wisdom of common sense. It's the compass that helps us navigate the unpredictable twists and turns of existence.

Remember my simple advice: take it one day at a time. Embrace the journey, for it's the sum of these days that make up your life. Cherish the friendships you've formed, for they are the ones who stand by your side through it all. Teach the next generation the value of being a good person, for their actions can shape a better world. Guide them to understand that common sense is not always common, but it's a beacon that can light their way in the darkest of times.

As we contemplate the absurdities and frustrations of our world, we must remember that change is possible. It may require revolutions of thought and action, but it is through collective efforts that we can hope to see a world guided by a more profound sense of common sense.

Despite all the complexities, life is worth living, and mistakes are part of our journey. Embrace the present, for yesterday has passed, and tomorrow is yet to come. Live in the moment, but don't forget to dream about the future. And always, always strive to be a good person, for in doing so, you make the world a better place.

So, dear reader, as you step away from the pages of this book and back into the world of everyday life, remember that common sense may not always be easy to find, but it's worth seeking. Laugh, shake your head, and enjoy the journey, for it is the only one you have.

9 781963 609011